REA

**ACPL ITEM
DISCARDED**

3 1833 04213 2263

D0949614

NOV 0 6 2002

Constance

Constance

A NOVEL

Catherine Cantrell

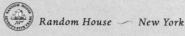 Random House New York

This is a work of fiction. All incidents, dialogues, and characters are products of the author's imagination and are not to be construed as real. In those few passages where actual place-names and well-known individuals are referred to, the situations, incidents, and dialogues described are entirely fictional and are not intended to depict actual events or to change the entirely fictional nature of the work. Any other resemblance to persons living or dead is entirely coincidental.

Copyright © 2002 by Catherine Cantrell

All rights reserved under International and Pan-American Copyright Conventions. Published in the United States by Random House, Inc., New York, and simultaneously in Canada by Random House of Canada Limited, Toronto.

RANDOM HOUSE and colophon are registered trademarks of Random House, Inc.

Library of Congress Cataloging-in-Publication Data
Cantrell, Catherine.
Constance : a novel / Catherine Cantrell.
p.   cm.
ISBN 0-375-50796-5 (acid-free paper)
1. Authors and publishers—Fiction.   2. Poetry—Authorship—Fiction.
3. New York (N.Y.)—Fiction.   4. Women editors—Fiction.
5. Women poets—Fiction.   I. Title.
PS3603.A59 C66 2002
813'.6—dc21   2001048980

Printed in the United States of America on acid-free paper
Random House website address: www. atrandom.com

2 4 6 8 9 7 5 3

First Edition

Book design by Mercedes Everett

To my mother

Constance

1

It is a subject open to endless speculation. How much of an artist's life can be seen in an artist's work? Was the *Mona Lisa* a painting of the wife of a Florentine merchant, or was she Leonardo's conception of the ideal woman? Did Flaubert model his Madame Bovary on an ill-fated doctor's wife named Delphine Couturier, or was she, as Flaubert famously claimed, a portrait of her creator? And how much of Emily Brontë's brother, Branwell, went into creating the indelible figure of Heathcliff in *Wuthering Heights*?

Even though I am not a scholar or an English professor but an editor, these questions have absorbed me, too. They spring to mind every time I find myself drawn to a work of art. They were on my mind when I first read the work of a young poet named Constance Chamberlain.

Constance, the woman who gives her name to this book, came into my life, it seemed to me, at a time when I needed to be brought back into life. My husband of seven years had died at the age of thirty-eight from a ruptured cerebral aneurysm. One moment we were sitting in a cab on our way home from the theater, the next moment he was holding his head in his hands with the worst headache of his life, then we were rushing to the hospital, and then he was gone. When Constance came to my attention, death was still in my heart. What I needed, and found in her, was a talent to take my mind off my troubles. She stood poised not only to enhance my already respectable list but to provide the balm that only engrossing work can bring.

I think in some ways, too, she reminded me a little of my husband, who had also been a writer. Like him, she was a conversationalist. My father had been one, too. All three of them possessed that rare ability to weave in and out of subjects like skilled craftsmen, creating colorful verbal tapestries as they went along. I was more of a listener, and I was comfortable in that role.

It is often said that most editors are failed writers. I have never thought of myself this way. I think editors have unique gifts, among them the ability to articulate weaknesses in a manuscript that a writer cannot quite pinpoint and the ability to sense when something is out of place, even if it is just a word or two. Writers, on the other hand, have gifts that I can't conceive of possessing, such as the power to create—the ability to make something out of nothing.

.   .   .

As a fiction and poetry editor at Peabody & Simms for more than ten years, I've had the privilege of working with many talented writers—providing direction, dispensing advice, bolstering egos, focusing ill-defined ideas, learning things I didn't know. In the process, friendships blossomed that required a great deal of care and feeding on my part, and I approached most of these relationships with excitement and enthusiasm. The better I knew my authors, I always reasoned, the better the work I could get out of them. So I learned how to ask the right questions, how to sit back and keep my opinions to myself, how to coax truth out of the guarded, shadowy regions of the human soul, and, most important, how to read between the lines. My open, nonjudgmental attitude seemed almost to invite confessions. I rarely had to dig very deeply before the riches of my writers' inner lives were revealed to me. Therefore, by the time I met Constance, a certain pride had grown in me at my ability to get the best out of anyone I set my sights on and honored with my attention.

But Constance was of a type that I thought had vanished from the arts long ago, a type I was not practiced in dealing with. For her, writing was not merely an act of self-expression but a religion, and her devotion was absolute. Her work was the indispensable cord that connected her to life. Consequently, the soil she grew in was not of a consistency that most people could have survived in for very long. It was severe and uncompromising, and my practiced warmth and understanding barely succeeded in scratching the surface.

If it hadn't been for a meddlesome newspaper reporter, I'm not sure I would ever have learned anything beyond what I could glean from the poetry she sent me. But in the end, her reserve softened by the hard exigencies of fate, the dam broke, and when it did break, it broke precipitately. She simply required more patience, more consideration, more understanding and active discernment than anyone I had ever worked with before.

Constance told me once that I was for her a magical stranger.

"And what is a magical stranger?" I asked.

"They're very common in fairy tales," she explained. "They're guides. Sometimes they're a dwarf, or a frog, or a white dove. And sometimes they are an editor."

That was the way she gave compliments. They came to you cloaked in metaphor or poetry. She never had any problems expressing her ideas. She was one of the most purely intellectual people I have ever known, but emotions were harder. They had to be dealt with indirectly, like an eclipse. If she had ever been forced to speak aloud about the inner workings of her own heart, I think she would have been struck dead.

Constance reminded me of the fragrant pink and white shrub roses that clung to the edge of my grandmother's garden. She seemed to thrive on neglect. At least I think it was the years of isolation and the rejection that spurred her on and inspired her to perfect her gifts. I still shudder to think what might have become of her if she had been discovered early and swept up into the publicity and media frenzy that now consume so many young writers' lives.

Her work and, even more important, her dedication also brought to mind something I had forgotten a long time ago: that artistic talent of any kind is exceedingly rare, and that beauty in art is not prized the way it once was. The idealism of my own early years had been worn down, by the time I met her, with a Brillo pad of defeated expectations. I had slowly learned to accept less and less.

As it was, I worked for the most respected publishing house in New York City: Peabody & Simms, the last major independent publisher in a much-beleaguered industry to be bought out by a conglomerate. Matthew Peabody IV, the great-grandson of the founder of the company, managed to keep the firm out of the hands of corporate raiders through the merger frenzy of the 1980s and early '90s, but competition from the corporate-owned houses, which could consolidate their production costs and overhead expenses, forced him to succumb in 1995. The battle Mr. Peabody had fought had earned him a great deal of respect and admiration from the old guard and among his staff, and whenever I saw the elder Peabody, whose son was now my boss, I couldn't help remembering the day he had come into our department to tell us the sad news. His brow damp with perspiration and his chalky-white eyebrows and hair a potent symbol of the life he had drained out of himself and funneled into the company, he made an enduring impression as the last of the gentleman publishers.

Mr. Peabody stayed on as president of the company under the new management—he lent the firm considerable cachet—and finally retired this past winter. His last few years were a struggle as he tried to help us adjust to the corporate mandates dictated from on high. Suddenly I found myself filling out a lot of forms with such offbeat names as "Balanced Business Score-card" and "Performance Index Review." Then we were enmeshed in something called "Best Practices," and people started disappearing. Work piled up and my hours lengthened. The pressure to make money and produce novelists with mass appeal increased, and the freedom to experiment diminished. It was as if all the pressures that Mr. Peabody had held at bay through the eighties and early nineties finally burst forth and engulfed us. Add to this the need to think about and respond in some way to the much-ballyhooed Internet, and the world around me seemed sometimes completely unrecognizable.

And it was when I had finally become largely inured to this new world that Constance appeared. It was just two years ago yesterday that I received a letter from her that ushered me into a universe of carefully modulated disclosures and disquieting devotion.

She gave the impression of being a fortress with a vast stockpile of intangible riches behind agonizingly high walls. The only way into her world was through her poetry, which led like a golden thread to the heart of the labyrinth.

The poetry, though, was only the thread. The real person, so long shut up behind her palace gates, perfecting her art and developing her mind, was hopelessly naïve about the politics involved in publishing. She harbored an antiquated notion that good work was *all* that mattered. That a pure voice would ring out among the stars. That people would have to pay attention. If only this were true, I used to think every time I had to disabuse her of some newly uncovered illusion.

And yet, there was a certain logic in her innocence that always made me stop and think. I suppose I had been in the industry too long and had seen too many mediocre authors elevated to international fame by the metallic maw of the publicity machine to believe any longer in anything so quaint as editorial guardianship. The idea that a natural talent might be cared for and developed until it grew to maturity was not something those of us in the profession thought about much anymore. Literary stars had to sprout in these financially conscientious times full grown from an unforgiving earth. Something in Constance's manner, though, drew this old-fashioned approach to writers out of me again and rekindled faded dreams.

It was snowing the day I received her letter. The temperature was hovering just above freezing, producing wet, soppy flakes that had threatened to soak through my new spring raincoat. It was the beginning of April, and the snowstorm had caught everyone off guard that morning and created the usual traffic delays and overcrowded subways. I remember all this so clearly because when I rushed into the office twenty-five minutes late, I failed to notice that Linda, my assistant, had already opened the morning mail and set it on my desk. As I struggled out of my coat, I absently laid my purse and wet umbrella down on the assortment of query letters, author inquiries, and memos she had left for me. By the time I realized what I had done, the letters on the top of the pile were damp, and I had to peel them apart. The letter on the very top was Constance's, her black felt-tip signature bleeding off the bottom of the page.

Linda always opened and sorted my mail for me. Unsolicited query letters and manuscripts went into the slush pile for her to sort through; letters and manuscripts from established authors, agents, and publishing colleagues came directly to me.

The letter from Constance had found its way into my pile because of a reference she made in it to my boss, Matthew Peabody V. She said she was writing to me on his recommendation, that they'd gone to the same school together, and that he'd spoken very highly of me.

She included a single poem with this letter that I have read so many times now I could recite it from memory:

A DIALOGUE IN SILENCE

The task complemented me
By what it unmasked of me.
Nobody knew me
Except the One who wooed me
With no relaxing.

The dark matters
Wiped out my mind
Like a bomb spent,
When I found the one
In whom his likeness met.

I was by spirits linked and circled
With this other's inner circle.
I had to leave it all unread.
My heart turned over
In its chamber of lead.

I was air, water, ground.
I had no voice, no sound.
Mute as a stranger standing by,
By this One, I think now, hypnotized.
The attraction bled.

But I have said,
And experience makes it true,
I found the One through the one who

3 1833 04213 2263

By his presence first
Made me aware of my maidenhood.

A dialogue in silence passed,
One for the other a looking glass.
The something he found I was made to see,
Though in the furthest hours,
When he was by then away from me.

By nature first in instincts cast,
Acting first and thinking last,
We made of him our enemy,
This One and me, with creatures massed.
Now I practice to redeem.

Words play for me the perfect host.
They form in me a destiny.
Their meaning with experience crossed,
The inner and the outermost
Together weave.

This was the One to me—
The back and forth, the repartee,
Synonymy and simile.
My mind slipped from its prisoner's chains
To inherit now a proper domain.

A world dewed with original light,
To requite me for the one of candlelight.

As on a pivot, the cosmos glows.
A piece of somebody's soul
Is still with me, though.

And that was how she insinuated herself into my busy life. Her words spoke to me like a voice in the darkness—lyrical, refined, almost painful in their beauty. Weary from years of having my senses assaulted with the monotonous drumbeat of half-assimilated, late-twentieth-century angst, I couldn't help listening.

·   ·   ·

After speaking with Matt and learning that she had indeed talked with him, and he had encouraged her to write to me, I contacted Constance and arranged to meet with her for lunch. And so, on a damp afternoon in the middle of April under cloud cover so heavy it threatened to extinguish all memory of the sun, we met at a French restaurant in Rockefeller Center called La Réserve. It was a very expensive French restaurant that I justified by telling myself that after staying in the office until ten o'clock for three weeks straight and eating mountains of Chinese takeout, I deserved a good meal on the house. Besides, she was a friend of Matt's, so I figured he couldn't complain.

I was seated at twelve-thirty and spent the next ten minutes watching the lunch crowd filter into the small dining room and studying the pastel murals of the only freshwater ponds in Jamaica Bay. These ponds were part of a wildlife refuge, or *réserve,* that gave the restaurant its name. Snow geese, herons, and ducks hovered against a powder-blue backdrop. Huge gold urns held a profusion of tall grasses and willow branches that seemed to have been picked from the very spot shown in the murals. Venetian-glass chandeliers served as a reminder of the sun.

At the table across from me sat the director of the Unterberg Poetry Center at the 92nd Street Y, one of New York's premier cultural institutions, and at the table next to him was the president of the New York Public Library with a man in an expensive Italian suit. I also noticed Oliver Browne, a well-known New York stage actor, on the other side of the room talking with his agent. All these faces were familiar ones and they highlighted for me something about New York that few people who haven't lived here know. New York is for all intents and purposes a small town. It's the kind of place where the famous and the not-so-famous live in such close proximity that the former elicit little more than passing notice from the latter. It's the kind of place where chance encounters could happen and did happen every day.

I looked at the front door again. Then, just as I was beginning to grow impatient, a young woman walked in. The way she held her hand to her chest for a moment told me she had been hurrying. I thought this must be Constance, and in my absorption at finally seeing her, my impatience subsided. I watched Jean-Louis Missud, the restaurant's managing partner and host, walk over to her, and the way he closed both hands over her hand when she extended it to him told me he was someone she had met many times before. This intrigued me. It wasn't what I had expected.

Jean-Louis helped her with her coat and shook out her umbrella, which was damp with rainwater. She wore a black short-sleeve bias-cut dress and black pumps. Her thin line and enviable posture reminded me of the dancers I sometimes saw wandering around Lincoln Center. I could tell by the way Jean-Louis and the waiters hovered around her that she was a restaurant favorite.

As she drifted toward me, I noticed she was wearing round diamond-stud earrings and a diamond pendant that I later came to see as a kind of trademark. Her skin was pale to the point of translucence and set off by wintry blue eyes and preternaturally rosy lips. The very whiteness of her skin made me think of the fine bone china my mother used to keep locked in the sideboard when I was a child. She seemed delicate and expensive and extremely well made.

As the waiter pulled out the table from the banquette, I extended my hand. "Hello, Ms. Chamberlain," I said. "I see you had no trouble finding the place."

She glanced around the room then as if she were taking in a thousand memories. "No, I didn't have any trouble finding it, but I am sorry I'm late. I forgot how bad the traffic is in midtown. I should have given myself more time. I apologize."

"It's all right," I assured her.

"I am sorry."

"It's fine."

She put a small black handbag and a leather portfolio down next to her. "I'm very happy to meet you," she said, observing me with an intensity that seemed to drive a steel beam up my spine.

"Likewise. Do you come here often?"

"Not often enough," she confided, and before I could follow

up on this enigmatic response, her attention had turned to the black tuxedoed waiter poised to take our drink order.

He greeted us with a deferential bow. "May I get you ladies something to drink?"

I looked at Constance. "I would like a glass of water with a slice of lemon, please," she said.

"I'll have a club soda with lime," I told him.

Moments later our drinks were in front of us, and the restaurant's large menus had been placed deftly in our hands. Constance studied the list of expertly crafted entrées, and offered her assessment of the Dover sole: "It's an experience of the highest order. Dreamlike. I recommend it without reservation."

"How can I resist a recommendation like that," I said. As an appetizer, she convinced me to order the lobster bisque, which I hadn't had for a long time. "It's famous," she said. "Or at least it should be."

After our menus were retrieved, she continued to scrutinize me with the kind of hopeful anxiety I imagined a prisoner might fix on a judge. Then the focus subsided as if she had willed herself into calmer waters, and she smiled.

"How long have you been writing, Ms. Chamberlain?"

"Since I was a child."

"I see." The poem she had sent me was at the front of my mind, and I praised her for it. "It's very beautiful." My compliment like a match lit a candle of expectation within her, and she glowed in the light of my approval. Her blue eyes grew almost iridescent.

It was a little disconcerting to see how much stock she put in my opinion when she knew me so little. I wondered what Matt had told her about me. I knew I was a very good editor, better than most, conscientious almost to a fault, ambitious, but I was not infallible. Nobody is, especially in this business where the criteria for success are so highly subjective.

"Did you bring some of your work with you?" I had asked her to do this when I'd spoken to her on the phone.

"Yes, I have it here." She opened the black portfolio, took out a thin white three-ring binder, and handed it to me.

I laid the binder on the table, opened it, and began to read. Her eyes were heavy upon me, but then she drew them away and directed her gaze toward the murals of herons and geese that had occupied me earlier. I tried to concentrate. It wasn't hard. The poems she had included were engrossing. Flashes of interest and beauty arrested my attention on every page. In each poem, there was something—a phrase, a line, a word, a rhythm, an insight, an image. There were no failures and one or two near masterpieces. My pulse quickened with the promise of her strange voice, and my absorption was so complete that I was taken aback to see a bowl of soup sitting on the table next to me when I finally looked up. Constance's soup sat untouched in front of her, and she sat as still and regal as a swan, with her hands folded neatly in her lap.

"These are very good."

"Thank you."

"I like the way you use words. Have you had any of these published?"

She shook her head.

"Have you sent them out to any of the magazines?"

She shook her head again.

"Really? Why?"

She shrugged. "I don't know. It seemed impractical."

"Impractical?"

"To have a poem published here or there. What is the point in that? I want them all to be together." She spoke of her poems as if she were talking about a family she didn't want to break up.

I sighed. "Let me explain to you how this business works, Ms. Chamberlain." I looked at the untouched bowl of lobster bisque in front of me.

She relaxed her posture slightly and quietly pulled a pad of paper and a pen out of her portfolio and set them next to her on the banquette. "That's fine, but shouldn't we eat our soup first?" she asked. "You wouldn't want it to get cold."

"No, I wouldn't."

She smiled and picked up her sterling silver spoon and dipped it into the creamy burnt-orange bisque. "I think this is the best soup in the city. Tell me what you think."

I tasted it. "It is good. It's very rich."

"I know. That's why I love it so. When you eat at a restaurant like La Réserve, you have to take time to really appreciate the food. You can't waste the experience."

"No, I guess you can't."

We ate our soup then in near silence as if we were attending Mass.

When she was done, she brought the corner of her napkin to her lips and then rearranged it neatly in her lap. After I had set my spoon down, she picked up her paper and pen.

I pushed my soup bowl aside. "Now I want to make it perfectly clear, Ms. Chamberlain—"

"Please call me Constance."

"Constance, then, that Peabody & Simms publishes a limited number of poetry books each year, and these books are always by poets who have established some sort of track record."

"I understand," she said. "And by track record you mean . . ."

"Publication in the magazines."

"I see."

I asked her for a piece of paper. "I'm going to write down a list of literary magazines that I think might be receptive to your work. You can look up their addresses in a book called *The International Directory of Little Magazines & Small Presses.* You can find it at most bookstores, or you can order it online."

"I've heard of it," she said.

I wrote down a list of ten or eleven magazines with a contact next to all but two of them. "Send 'A Dialogue in Silence' to Adrian Regent at *Pen & Paper,* and use my name by way of introduction. You can use my name with all these submissions. That should ensure you a reading at least."

I was particularly keen to have Constance send what I considered her best poem to Adrian Regent, the splashy poetry editor at *Pen & Paper,* New York's oldest arts and culture magazine and a still vital, if somewhat diminished, cultural arbiter. Adrian had just published an article in *The Poetry Journal* on the need to promote new talent. I thought the article was a trifle disingenuous because *Pen & Paper* was notorious for publishing second-rate poetry by established novelists for whom poetry was little more than a diversion. Still, I wanted to see if Adrian might recognize Constance's talent. If she did, and I knew the chances were slim, it might help me make a case for Constance at Peabody & Simms.

I handed her the completed list, and she wrote *"The Interna-tional Directory of Little Magazines"* at the bottom of the sheet.

"How many should I send to each editor?"

"Three or four, depending on their length."

She wrote "three or four poems each."

"Should I send different poems to each editor?"

"Yes."

"And what about cover letters? Should I send a cover letter?"

"You'll have to send a short one if you're going to mention my name."

"Yes, of course," she added quickly.

"Now, I want to tell you something, Constance. Many edi-tors have tin ears when it comes to poetry nowadays, so don't expect too much."

"But, Ms. Clifford," she said, her eyes igniting with hope once again, "I got your attention, didn't I?"

"Yes, you did," I admitted, "but . . ."

"But you're not ordinary."

"I wouldn't say that."

She smiled at me. "I did my homework, Ms. Clifford." I told her to call me Morgan. "I've examined many of the books you've edited, Morgan. In almost every one, the author men-tions you by name and thanks you. That means something."

It was true. Many of my authors, thankful for my time and attention, had been kind enough to mention me in their ac-knowledgments. It was about the highest compliment an editor could receive.

I could tell by the self-assured, almost serene expression on her face that she saw our coming together as nothing less than an act of God. Fate and destiny pulled up their chairs next to us and remained as silent but powerful companions during the rest of our time together. I could feel their influence in the way she talked about her literary heroes: Emily Brontë, Emily Dickinson, Anton Chekhov, Theodore Dreiser, F. Scott Fitzgerald, and Sylvia Plath. It was as if each one of them had instructed her personally—as if she were a very small but important part of a vast continuum. There was an intimacy there that made me think of Emily Dickinson's devotion to the novels of George Eliot, or F. Scott Fitzgerald's respect for Willa Cather, or even Rilke's idolization of Rodin. Her love for these writers was all-consuming.

She talked at length about *The Great Gatsby* and told me that the preface to Joseph Conrad's *The Nigger of the 'Narcissus'* had been instrumental in shaping Fitzgerald's ideas about fiction. "Fitzgerald wrote in a letter to Ernest Hemingway that 'the purpose of a work of fiction is to appeal to the lingering after-effects in the reader's mind.' I believe in that conception of art—specifically as it applies to poetry." She was also particularly fond of the following line in one of Emily Dickinson's letters: "The Astounding subjects are the only ones we pass unmoved." She couldn't get it out of her mind, she told me, since she'd read it last summer.

"Constance," I said, when I could finally get a word in edgewise, "may I ask you something?"

She nodded.

"Have you ever attended a workshop?" Many of the young writers whose manuscripts found their way onto my desk either had attended a series of writing workshops or had their MFAs from places like Iowa or Columbia.

"No," she said firmly.

"I'm not suggesting that you should," I added. "I was only wondering."

"Why?"

"Why was I wondering?"

She nodded again.

"Because you've taken a very nontraditional route. People make a lot of connections in these workshops and MFA programs. It's not just about writing."

"Yes, but you see it *is* only about writing, or it should be. I don't want to take one of those classes and lull myself into thinking that I'm competing with a bunch of people in a workshop. I would never deceive myself in that way. Writers, if they are any good at all, will ask themselves, every time they sit down to write, if they are capable of being as good as a Fitzgerald or a Dickinson or a Chekhov. Not *the same as,* but as good as. They have to have an inviolate personal vision. I would think being in a workshop would expose you to too many people's opinions. You might compromise yourself without even seeing what you were doing. No, I would never do it."

The way she talked about workshops, you would have thought I'd just asked her if she had ever considered doing hard drugs or becoming a prostitute. The force of her argument was humbling.

As the soup bowls were cleared away and our silver-domed entrées placed before us, I asked her if she thought there was anything indispensable to becoming a writer.

"Time," she said without hesitation. "You have to separate yourself from the world, finally, and think. That's why I admire a writer like Emily Dickinson. She had the courage to do that."

"And did you do that?"

"I tried to," she said. "For five years I focused on my writing pretty much to the exclusion of everything else."

"It's harder today, isn't it? I mean, financially."

"Yes, it's a lot harder."

When the lunch was over, I paid the bill, and after retrieving our coats and umbrellas we walked outside. It was raining now with a force that seemed wholly out of proportion to anything one might deem a spring shower. We stood underneath the white awning in front of the restaurant, and she thanked me for my kindness and advice.

"I'll be in touch. I'll send my poems out right away." Her eyes were glistening now, clear blue pools of water stirred by a breeze of anticipation—of summer, of success, of dreams fulfilled. Her unrestrained belief in the future suspended for a moment my own doubts about the hard road that lay ahead of her.

She reached out her hand, and, touched by her innocence, I squeezed it. "Good luck," I said. "Let me know what happens."

This last comment seemed to disappoint her, as if it had not been necessary.

"Of course I will," she said.

She opened her black umbrella then and, gathering her coat close around her long neck, plunged into the rain. As I watched her walk away, a feeling of doom crept over me, and as the crowd closed in around her, my thoughts turned to the Emily Dickinsons and van Goghs of this world who never had a chance during their lifetimes to see and experience the public face of fame.

2

I hadn't realized how jaded the years of focusing obsessively on the bottom line and fighting corporate bureaucracy had left me. In the weeks that followed that initial lunch, every time I thought about Constance I could feel again that romantic flame of hope ignite new thoughts and ways of looking at things. I was reminded of all my early aspirations and promise, and I felt as if I were starting all over again. Things she had said that day kept going through my mind: "A work of art is a miracle, something that should never have been. That's why true art is always unexpected and yet unmistakable. It feels as if something distinctly felt, but only dimly apprehended, has been pulled out of the air and made real." "The structure of a great poem or novel goes far beyond the words that make up the poem or novel." "The film *Excalibur* is a dramatization of an *inner* process. All myths are." And then there was this tidy little aphorism: "Beware of the man in whom the good and evil are not well mixed." She said she had derived this from something she'd read in *The Complete Prose and Poetry of William Blake*. "I never trust people," she told me, "who are *suspiciously* good."

We also talked about our greatest fear. Mine was very

mundane—death. "I don't fear death," she said, "at least not my own death. What I fear most is the loss of the imagination." She said *the* imagination not *my* imagination, as if her creativity were intimately tied up with the rest of the universe. She explained then that this was what T. S. Eliot had been writing about in such poems as *The Waste Land* and the *Four Quartets.* "Eliot, Fitzgerald, Sylvia Plath, they saw it coming—this deathly alienation from the wellsprings of life. They straddled both worlds. But now, people don't even remember that there was a time when it was possible to live through your imagination— when your own psychology invested the world with meaning. Today everything is far too concrete and literal." And then she added, after a pause that drew her eyes away from me toward an invisible world only she could see, "If your imagination burns out, you quietly burn out with it."

.   .   .

Almost three months passed without word from her, except for a handwritten thank-you note I received a few days after our lunch. Then one afternoon while I was sitting at my desk reviewing cover art for a new novel, Linda came in with a packet of letters. They were paper-clipped together, and there was a short handwritten note on top:

Dear Morgan:

I followed your instructions and sent out my poetry to the magazines you suggested. As you can see, I got some very nice rejection letters, but no acceptances. In most cases, my work was simply "not appropriate."

Thank you for your help. If you have any further advice on how I might proceed, I would be very glad to hear it. I realize how busy your schedule is, but I have no one else to ask.

Thank you again for your time and consideration. I appreciate it very much.

All my best,
Constance

P.S. You said at lunch that Emily Dickinson was one of your favorite poets, so I'm enclosing an essay I wrote about her a couple of years ago. I thought you might like it.

I pulled Adrian Regent's letter out of the pile. *Pen & Paper's* familiar letterhead with the oval seal of a 1920s flapper made me think of the countless careers this magazine had made and broken. I could almost feel the exclusivity in the touch of the cream-colored rag paper. The letter was already a month old. "Dear Ms. Chamberlain," it read:

Thank you for giving us the opportunity to see your work. I've read the poems carefully and found them intriguing, if not quite right for *Pen & Paper*. I wish I had better news and had more time to go into detail—not that you need critiquing, of course.

Thank you for thinking of us. I wish you all the best.

Sincerely,
Adrian Regent

I put down the letter and pulled the latest copy of *Pen &*
Paper out of my overloaded in-box and flipped to the table of
contents. All three poems in that week's edition were by the
same familiar writers. The first two poems, one by a veteran
teacher of creative-writing workshops, the other by a chronicler
of middle-aged ennui, left me numb. The third one, by a pet of
the awards circuit who had once been a member of a Los Angeles gang called Stoned Angels, unsettled my stomach. Sufficient
to say, the recurring motif in this ex–gang member's poem,
which was entitled "Roaming Holiday," was coyote piss. There
was not a hint of music in it, no arresting ideas, nothing of
beauty or sublimity. The writer had arranged the words on the
page in the shape of a coyote's profile in a vain attempt to show
how clever he could be.

I put the magazine aside and picked up the short essay she
had sent me. It was entitled "Emily Dickinson: Naked Obscurity." It was about the price Dickinson paid in being forced to
live in the shadows despite her prodigious talent. It was extremely well written and carefully argued, but at the same time
there was something about it that made me uneasy. I suspect it
had to do with the implicit sense of identification that ran
through the piece. *I never think of Emily Dickinson as the eccentric*
most people think her to be. Maybe because some part of me, for better
or worse, understands her perfectly.

Emily Dickinson was the most famous and respected female
poet in the canon, and since there were so few female poets to
begin with, it was natural for any young female poet to try to
identify with her. But her ascetic lifestyle was not one that encouraged the development of the personality in all its dimen-

sions. It might have been the best lifestyle for Emily Dickinson in nineteenth-century Amherst, Massachusetts, when marriage meant endless pregnancies and a house full of children, with no time to write, but it was not right or necessary for a young woman at the end of the twentieth century to live this way— isolated, alone, and closed off from the world. I wasn't sure if Constance understood this. I hoped she did, but I thought maybe she didn't, and I was surprised to find how much this concerned me.

Isolation of the type Emily Dickinson experienced can lead to certain kinds of insights, Constance pointed out in her essay, *that might not be possible in a life more fully integrated with its surroundings. The weight of the inner world becomes heavy when so much time is spent walking through its garden paths and dimly lit corridors. As with eyes trained to see in the dark, strange, obscure shapes become visible and then familiar.* I think she might have been speaking about this when she wrote:

> *One need not be a Chamber—to be Haunted—*
> *One need not be a House—*
> *The Brain has Corridors—surpassing*
> *Material Place—*

I had worked with many haunted writers before. The impulse to write is for the most part an impulse to understand, and the thing most writers want to understand, above all other things, is where they came from. But this process also works in reverse. Whenever I read anything that is exceptional or even just beautifully written, I also want to understand. I want to understand where the poem or novel or short story came from, and I was beginning to want to understand very much where Constance came from.

The price Emily Dickinson paid, willingly or not, when she chose the life she did for herself was loneliness. She had ecstasy, rapture, and joy, but she was always alone. There is no greater loneliness in life than that of not being understood—it is the flower out of which all madness blooms.

I put down her essay and thought about Emily Dickinson's failure to interest Thomas Wentworth Higginson, a contributing editor at the *Atlantic Monthly* and one of the few editors she sent her poetry to, in publishing her work. His reply to the first batch of poems she sent him has not survived, but he apparently told her that her "gait" was "spasmodic" and recommended that she "delay to publish." I took solace, therefore, in the fact that things had not changed that much in the last century and a half. It was still just as hard as it had been then.

I picked up her essay and circled the line about loneliness and madness.

Then, despite looming deadlines and meetings, I sat very still in my ergonomically designed office chair and began to think. I knew I could tell Constance to keep sending out her poetry. Some magazine somewhere was bound to publish one of her poems sometime. But then what? She was obviously not going to be embraced by the cadre of poetry editors guarding the gates of the establishment. Their ears were tuned now to a frequency that didn't pick up the signals she was sending out. I'd never be able to make a case at Peabody & Simms for an unknown poet with no publishing history whatsoever. And besides, there was simply too much noise out there for her to be heard even if I could publish her. The barriers to success seemed insurmountable until my eye fell again on the sentence I had circled with my felt-tip marker: *There is no greater loneliness in life than that of not being understood—it is the flower out of which all madness blooms.*

That sentence followed me around for a week as I turned various ideas over in my head.

A few days later, I had Constance standing before me in my office. She was wearing a pink tailored suit, and the diamond pendant I had admired at lunch was visible against her pale white skin. I told her to have a seat.

"Thank you for following up with me on the poems you sent out," I began. "I'm sorry the magazines weren't more responsive, but I did warn you not to expect too much."

"I know," she said, "but I did expect too much. I read all the magazines you put on the list and tried to send them poems that would meet their requirements, but . . ." She shrugged as if she didn't know quite what to make of the rejections.

"It's curious, isn't it?" she added.

"What is?"

"That they publish some of the poems they publish."

I would have liked more than anything to have been able to give her a logical explanation, but I had none.

"Do you think perhaps it has something to do with politics? With politics taking precedence over art?"

"Probably," I said.

"A lot of these writers seem to have an agenda."

"I know."

"I think maybe I've focused too much on the classics. I haven't read enough contemporary poetry."

"It is important to understand the current market," I said.

"Yes, I see that now. But I thought . . ." Again her eyes drifted away from me as if her attention had been caught up in the exigencies of her perplexed psyche.

"You thought what?"

"I thought if you're going to be a writer, you have to measure yourself against the very best of what's gone before you. If you can't meet that standard, I don't see what the point is."

"The point?"

"The point in being a writer. What kind of contribution can you make if you're not building on the past? In my poetry, I always attempt to explore inner experiences I do not think have been put down on paper before."

Her purity of purpose was as admirable as it was naïve. Did she really think all writers approached their work in this way? Had she never read any of the articles about six-figure advances for writers of murder mysteries and crime capers? I couldn't bring myself to ask.

"Constance," I said gently, "you're looking at this world of publishing very idealistically."

She fixed me then with solemn eyes so burdened with disappointment that I had to restrain myself from laughing.

"Do you really think so?" she asked.

"Yes, I think so, but time and experience will remedy that."

She had been perched on the edge of her chair with her hands folded in her lap and her ankles crossed under the chair.

She sat back now and a languid attentiveness settled into her slender body.

"To be honest with you, Constance, poetry is actually written more than it's read nowadays, and when it is read, it tends to be read by other poets and academicians. It's frustrating, but that's the way it is. Robert Frost was the last poet in this country to find a popular audience and to make a living as a poet. Maybe you already knew this."

She raised her eyebrows and shook her head slowly. I gathered that because she read poetry, and because it played a vital role in her life, she assumed it held the same precedence of place in other people's lives.

"What I'm proposing is that we integrate the poems you've written within the context of a novel. First novels are much easier to sell than poetry books."

She was staring at me now—her face calm, her eyes unblinking, her brow smooth, her mouth immobile. It seemed futile to try to discern her reaction, so I pushed on.

"About ten years ago, the English novelist A. S. Byatt wrote a book called *Possession,* which was filled with poetry—imitation Victorian poetry, but poetry nevertheless. This novel found a very large audience. It was a bestseller on both sides of the Atlantic and brought Byatt considerable fame."

Her eyes left me and wandered around the room. I could almost see the gears shifting in her mind. Then her eyes came back to me and she sighed. In her quiet, subdued manner she communicated almost a feeling of boredom, but I knew she was listening. I had a strong intuition then that trying to write a novel would force her to widen her perspective and take in more of the world around her. Whatever came of it, I thought it would be good for her.

"What are you thinking? Do you see what I'm driving at? Is this a plausible idea?"

"It's fine, but I don't write novels."

"But you could try."

She brought the tips of her fingers together in a gesture of prayer and lowered her head. Finally, she looked up and said, with some of her habitual enthusiasm seeping back into her voice, "It's not unprecedented. F. Scott Fitzgerald and James Joyce integrated their poetry into their first novels."

"There you go."

"But they were novelists, not poets."

"So we'll reverse the process. You'll be a poet who integrates a novel into her poetry."

Her blue eyes caught a ray of light from the window behind me and a gleam of hope issued forth. She smiled slowly.

"I'll tell you what made me think of it. The language in your essay is beautiful. If you can write like that, you can write a novel."

She continued to weigh my words, and then, as if something had moved between us like an eclipse, her mood darkened.

I began talking again in an effort to bring back the light. "Constance, to be a novelist requires the ability to penetrate human psychology. There was one sentence in your essay in particular that convinced me you have this facility. Do you know which one I'm thinking about?"

She shook her head.

"It's this one," I said, picking up her Emily Dickinson essay and flipping to the marked page, *"There is no greater loneliness in life than that of not being understood—it is the flower out of which all madness blooms.* That's a thought-provoking line. I've never looked at loneliness or madness in quite that way before. I've been thinking about it all week."

"That's nice," she said absently, as she dropped into her own thoughts again. She was staring at a pearl ring on the middle finger of her left hand. Then she looked up at me again.

"But you also have to be able to tell a story," she pointed out, "and I'm not a storyteller. I'm someone who records impressions, passing scenes, momentary states of being."

"But have you ever tried to write a novel before?"

I took her silence as a no.

"So, would it hurt you to try?"

I thought about her poetry again and her unyielding devotion to the art form.

"Isn't it at least worth trying for the sake of your poetry? You don't want to end up like Emily Dickinson, do you? Unknown and unappreciated in her lifetime."

"Except by her close friends."

"Yes, well, fine, but . . ."

"No, I know. You're right. I'll try. I can't promise you anything, but I'll try."

"That's all I can ask."

She eyed me for a moment. "So I'll be your experiment."

"Yes, I've needed an experiment for a while."

"How much time do I have?"

"As much time as you need."

She looked around the room again as if she were silently

communing with a roomful of invisible companions. "Well, I guess I better be going. I'm sure you have work to do."

We stood up.

"I'll see you out," I said.

As we traversed the long, narrow hallway toward the metal fire door that led to the reception area, she grew more and more pensive. She was walking right next to me, but I could feel her thoughts moving farther and farther away with each step we took. When I pushed open the door for her, she passed by me and said "Thank you" as if she were speaking to a stranger. I pressed the elevator button and then turned to say good-bye. Her eyes were now brimming with emotion, and her hand was extended in thanks. Fully present once more, she said, with a candor that drew me back on myself, "Thank you for believing in me. Besides my mother, you're only the second person who has done that." She shook my hand firmly and stepped into the crowded car. Then the doors slid closed, and she was gone.

From that day forward I thought of Constance, unlike my other writers, as a special project; even, to use her word, as an experiment. I felt it would have been unconscionable on my part simply to let her sink into oblivion. There was a flame of real talent in her heart that needed only to be fanned into a luminous blaze. I would simply direct her creativity into an acceptable form without compromising the integrity of her poetry. I had always wondered what kind of marvelous novel a poet like Emily Dickinson might have written. I envisioned Constance walking in one day with some never-before-seen concept in a form that would utterly floor people with its originality.

3

Months went by, and the promise of summer turned to the foreboding of autumn without word from Constance, except, of course, for her customary thank-you note, which I received a few days after our meeting. My schedule intensified as we got ready to introduce the spring list, and pressure from the corporate offices to increase sales volume forced me to take on a couple of John Grisham wanna-bes who required an inordinate amount of hand-holding. Constance never completely left my thoughts, though. I'd see pieces of her face in people I passed on the street, on the covers of magazines, in advertisements and on billboards. Things she had said would come back to me, too, as I was reading manuscripts or flipping through *The New York Times Book Review*. Her exacting standards began to influence me, and I found myself looking at fiction in an even more discriminating way than I had before, asking myself before all other questions—before marketing opportunities and sales potential—what contribution a particular piece of work might make to the art form. Needless to say, almost all of the manuscripts I reviewed and books I examined had little to recommend them under these uncompromising terms.

Sometimes I'd catch myself in the middle of a daydream I thought I had relinquished long ago. It had to do with Maxwell Perkins, the famous Scribner's editor who oversaw the careers of such literary luminaries as F. Scott Fitzgerald and Ernest Hemingway. I would imagine myself sitting in the old Scribner Building on Fifth Avenue behind Perkins's high, spacious lecternlike desk writing out my editorial comments with a fountain pen. I envied Maxwell Perkins because he had achieved, by brilliantly but humbly doing his job, a kind of immortality. As long as people continued to read Fitzgerald and Hemingway, his name would remain in the public consciousness. Even the editorially challenged Thomas Wentworth Higginson had become a permanent part of literary history simply because Emily Dickinson had chosen to write to him instead of some other editor. I longed to be so anointed.

I had gotten into publishing because I loved books more than anything else in the world and wanted, when I graduated from New York University, to extend that love affair into my adult life. My father had been a professor of American literature at Yale and had introduced me to the raptures of reading early. When I was growing up, he used to take me to the Beinecke Rare Book and Manuscript Library on campus to look at the letters and manuscripts of writers like James Joyce and Edith Wharton. A New Critic through and through, my father taught me that literary works have an objective integrity that must be respected. If I wrote a paper for one of my English classes that seemed, in his mind, overly subjective, he would ask me,

"Where exactly does the novel say that, Morgan?" And then he would become very stern and remind me that "you cannot make a work of art mean what you want it to mean." He also had little use, beyond the mere outline of a writer's life, for biographical details. He thought they were of limited value in understanding a writer's work. I suppose in reaction to my father's rather obstinate views in this regard, and because I am by nature an inquisitive person, I've always gone out of my way to learn as much as possible about the lives of writers I love. I want to know everything, and I find infinite pleasure in being able to see the way a writer transforms a personal incident from his or her life into a poem or novel with universal significance. For me, that is the true miracle of literature.

My father had been thrilled when I'd decided to go into publishing, and whenever I saw him, he would bombard me with questions about my work. He always wanted to know if I had made any "exciting new discoveries." He had a penchant for talent and almost a sixth sense for picking out the challenging individual in a crowded room. I think the greatest disappointment of my father's life was the fact that he'd never had a protégé, someone whose potential he could work with and develop to the full. He'd had many bright students at Yale, but bright in the conventional meaning of that word. That is, they could do the work, they could give him what he asked for, they could write solid and well-argued papers. But that wasn't enough for my father; he wanted something beyond this. My father looked for passion in his students, for a love of literature to match his own. But as the years went by, more and more of his students were simply passing through his English classes on their way to busi-

ness and law school. They weren't interested in making literature their life. And the ones who were, he said, had little to recommend them. "They all want to be *deconstructionists*," I often
heard him say.

So, perhaps to redress this injustice, and ameliorate my father's disappointment, I set my sights on a similar goal. The first
day I walked into Peabody & Simms as a lowly editorial assistant
and sat down at my metal desk in the mucky yellow hallway
outside my editor's office, I made a vow to myself that one day
I would pluck a gifted writer from obscurity and provide the
editorial guidance necessary to ensure lasting fame. For years
the identity of this writer had been very fuzzy. Man or woman?
Young or old? American or foreign-born? My imagination had
not discriminated. The only thing I had been absolutely sure of
was that I would know this person when they walked into my
life. They would radiate some sort of energy that would, like a
talisman, mark them unmistakably.

Constance's purity of purpose drove this dream out of hiding, and I found myself anticipating the future with renewed
hope.

I also became curious about her.

She had never said one word to me about her private life—
no fleeting mention of a husband or boyfriend, a marriage or a
divorce, nothing about her upbringing, her family, brothers or
sisters. The only thing that had even approached a personal
revelation was that brief expression of gratitude in the reception area before she stepped onto the elevator, when she'd
said, "Except for my mother, you're only the second person to believe in me." Not much could be deduced from this except that

she'd received a certain measure of maternal affection. And if I was only the second person to believe in her, who was the first? And why hadn't there been more? She was a beautiful young woman, talented, intellectually gifted, and charming. It didn't make sense.

I examined the poems she had left with me for clues.

There was a knowingness in much of her work about the illusionary aspects of romantic love, especially the false sense of intimacy and understanding that can be engendered by the appearance of a pretty girl. These poems felt to me like the cool comments of a woman who is five steps ahead of everyone around her.

A PLACE IN HIS DREAMS

So you've resigned me to your dreams.
I suppose that was the easiest thing for you to do.
It has been done before.
Men love the fantasy of me—
Someone who will bring out their deepest
      emotions
And give them a good reason for living.

I wonder sometimes what it is that I do.
There is nothing that intriguing about me.
I'm just an ordinary girl.
Perhaps I'm beautiful—
Something you want to touch—
And I keep a lot of things in my mind,

But a lot of people do.
Maybe it's in the way I combine the two.
Someone once told me it was an extraordinary
    blend.
After seven years, I split his heart in two.
Without knowing how,
I found a way inside.

The interior of his house was dark.
There was only a single candle by his bedside.
He said he'd found me in the flames.
At night, when his house was especially quiet,
I came to him.
And every morning, he said,
He was never quite the same.

She seemed to turn the assertion that Edgar Allan Poe had made in his "Philosophy of Composition" that "the death of a beautiful woman is, unquestionably, the most poetical topic in the world" inside out. She frequently took the persona of such women, but her perspective was not the perspective of the admiring lover or mystified observer imagining what such a woman is feeling, but of the woman herself. It was in this exploration of an inner experience—an inner experience examined by few—that I thought she offered something new. I had always known that physical attractiveness automatically conferred power, especially in the lives of women, but I'd never seen it laid out in such a bald-faced manner before.

SEEING THROUGH ME

You said I had intelligence,
Beauty.
You said my heart drew at least
One ocean in—

That there was a vastness to me—
The scope of the sky.
But I, for my part,
Encompass a daily life.

I'm quiet about the things I see,
Equivocal,
But I'll accept
Whatever it is you want to take out of me.

If you need something beautiful,
Then that's what I'll be.
But just remember,
My load will be heavier than most.

You don't want to kill me.

And, finally, the following poem confirmed in my own mind
the vision I had projected onto her of a princess living in a kind
of lonely, intense splendor:

Catherine Cantrell

MY DISTANT GARDEN

I stand alone
In a distant garden
Covered with vines like the palace
Sleeping Beauty lay charmed in.
No one lives here except me
And the gatekeeper,
Who, respecting my wishes,
Bears me no mind.
He periodically inspects my estate,
Passing through my flowers
But never questioning my fate.
He prides himself
That no intruder
Has ever been permitted
To pass through his gate.
I respect him,
And when I venture out of my garden,
I tell him always
Exactly when I'll return.
I never come home late.

One Friday afternoon, when my powers of concentration
were completely spent after a long and arduous week, I walked
down the hall and knocked on Matt Peabody's door. Matt was
my boss, although only a few years before he had been simply
my colleague. He now had a corner office replete with a Chippendale mahogany partners desk and matching bookcases he

had bought himself, a leather sofa, prominently displayed plaques and awards, and an assortment of potted plants. Still, despite all these accoutrements, it was impossible to disguise the fact that he was enclosed within the same mucky yellow walls that bound me. Matt had occupied the office next to mine when he'd been editor of our business and history lists, and we'd quickly struck up a friendship that had cooled somewhat, but not disappeared, since he'd been promoted to editor in chief. He'd taken me aside when his promotion had been announced and told me, very solemnly, that in order to establish his authority and not appear to be playing favorites, our frequent lunches and gab sessions would have to be curtailed. I smiled when he told me this, bowed, and backed out of the room.

Part of me knew, though, that he hadn't meant any offense. Matt was the fifth generation of Peabodys to be in the publishing business—a business that didn't really suit him. He would have preferred to be down on Wall Street, working in one of the investment banks where he could indulge his love of pure numbers. But fate had made him a Peabody, and the Peabodys were a tightly knit clan who adhered to the wishes of their elders. As his father's only son, he was bound to continue in the family business.

I knocked on his open door. "Are you too busy to talk to an old friend?" I said.

He looked up and waved me in.

"Where is Helen?" I asked as I settled into one of the two damask-upholstered armchairs across from his desk. "Why isn't she guarding the gates?" Helen was his secretary, and she was very protective of him. No one was allowed to cross his threshold without first going through her.

"She had a dentist appointment. She left early."

Matt's black and gold Montblanc fountain pen—a gift from his grandfather—was poised over a pile of reports.

"I want to ask you some questions," I told him.

"About what?"

"Your friend."

"My friend?"

"Constance."

"Ah, yes, Constance." He carefully placed his pen on his desk. "You want me to tell you about Constance."

"Yes, that's what I want you to do."

He sat back in his black leather office chair. His platinum monogrammed cuff links competed for attention with his red silk tie. There was a dreamy glint in his eyes that I had never seen there before, and I found myself staring at him for a moment as if he weren't Matt at all but only a curious imposter.

"I met with her again."

"You met her again?"

"Yes. She's rather intriguing."

He leaned his head back and glanced up at the ceiling.

"And she can write," I told him. "I'm impressed."

He was looking at me now.

"Did she write in college?" I asked, trying to find some way into their shared past.

"Yes, she did, but she never showed anyone anything."

"Never?"

"No, she was very private." The moony, reverential look in

his eyes had permeated his whole face now, and a youthful glow emanated from his well-shaven features.

"Did she ever talk about what she was writing?"

He shook his head.

I considered this information for a moment. It seemed right in line with everything I had learned about her so far.

"She's surprisingly naïve about the publishing world," I told him. "She was dismayed when I had her send out her poems to the little magazines and they were all rejected. She was really taken aback."

He smiled. "She was always pretty naïve."

"So, what was your relationship to her in college?"

He looked up at the ceiling again and brought the pads of his fingers together one by one, as if he were counting something in his head. "We were chums," he began, and then leveled me with his pale green eyes, *"her* word."

"Chums?"

"That's right."

"Was it mutual?" I asked.

He leaned forward and picked up his pen again. "What do you mean?"

"Were you mutual chums?"

Matt looked at me steadily. He was married now to a woman he had met on a trip to the Hamptons, and had a three-year-old daughter. "Pretend we're back in the old days," I said, "before your big promotion. You would have told me anything back then." I got up and shut the door. "It doesn't go out of this room."

He shook his head. "There isn't anything to tell."

"Nothing?"

His eyes fell then, and he became suddenly fascinated with his Montblanc pen, turning it over in his hands and studying its smooth, polished exterior. "Not nothing. There was always something. Even if you could never understand exactly what it was." He smiled to himself. "I've tried to figure it out. She was . . . very understanding." He was now talking more to himself than to me, and I sat back in my chair.

"It's funny when you look back," he said dreamily. "It's funny that I can look back now. I guess I'm getting older. I read something in the *Times Magazine*. Jay McInerney was talking about the eighties. He said it was a more innocent time, but he was wrong. It wasn't. No, my generation . . . we were many things, but we were never innocent. The drugs, the drinking, the boredom we felt, the fact that nothing could shock us. Maybe that's why Constance stood out. She was like, I don't know, a daisy. As innocent as they come. I remember the first time I saw her. It was at the beginning of the year." He laughed. "She was a freshman. We were juniors."

"We?"

"My roommate and I."

"Your roommate Hutchins?"

"Yes."

"The one I offended because I kept calling him by his last name?"

He nodded.

"What was his first name again?"

"Nick."

"Oh, right." When I first started working at Peabody &

Simms, before I met my husband, I often did things with Matt outside of work. We used to take long walks through Central Park, and I'd listen to him talk about the anxiety of being a Peabody and his overarching fear that he would never know if his accomplishments in life were simply the result of his birthright or his own talents. "I'll never know," he used to say over and over again, "I'll never know if I could have done it on my own." It was a different perspective from the one I was used to. I was from that large, nameless mass of people who simply wonder if they will ever have the chance to make it, to see if they have what it takes. I was a striver. Matt was a member of the American aristocracy. He had money. He had a name. Besides Peabody & Simms, his family owned a small magazine empire and an extensive collection of rare manuscripts and first editions and an impressive art collection of modernist masterpieces that was worth millions. He was used to seeing his family name plastered all over the city.

In those early days, Matt was always talking about his friend Hutchins, who lived in Boston and worked for a pharmaceutical company. It was always "Hutchins this" and "Hutchins that." I never thought of his having any other name except Hutchins, so when he finally came down one weekend to see Matt, and Matt introduced me to him as Nick, I couldn't make the adjustment in my mind, and the whole weekend I kept calling him Hutchins. Matt finally pulled me aside and said I was really beginning to annoy Nick with this Hutchins business, but I just couldn't stop it.

"And you were all friends?" I asked.

"In a manner of speaking."

"What do you mean?"

"Yeah, we were friends. Constance and I were good friends at one time."

"But you are still friends, aren't you?"

"Yes, but not the way we used to be."

"Why not?"

He shrugged.

"Did something happen? Why didn't you ever mention her to me before?"

He lowered his head. "I tried to protect her," he said.

"Protect her from what?"

"My roommate was not . . ." He seemed to be searching for exactly the right word. "Honorable."

I smiled. "I've never heard you use that word before."

He looked at me.

"Honorable," I echoed. I wanted to laugh. Matt had regaled me over the years with stories about his wild college days. I didn't know where this was coming from. "Since when did you start being concerned with people being honorable? I thought there was supposed to be a cold, calculating Wall Street shark lurking underneath that gentlemanly exterior," I said. But I could see that he had been. The downcast look on his face told me so. At one time he had been concerned with being honorable. He'd been very concerned about it indeed.

"He wasn't right for her," he said defensively. "He didn't appreciate her at all. It was better that they didn't end up together. I'm sure of it."

"That who didn't end up together?"

"Nick and Constance."

"Nick and Constance? They went together?"

He nodded.

"Really?" I said, thoroughly taken aback. I tried to picture it. The Nick Hutchins I had met was certainly handsome, but his rather pedestrian outlook blunted his appeal considerably for me. I had no luck engaging him in conversation that went beyond anything but the most superficial generalizations. The most interesting thing he said all weekend had to do with the high cost of prescription drugs. He said that if they reduced prices, it would cut into company profits, which would decrease the amount of money spent on research and development, which would reduce the number of drugs available to extend and, in some cases, save people's lives. For some reason, I remembered that. Maybe because I had never looked at it that way before. What was so curious about him was that he appeared to be completely comfortable simply staring off into space. There was no awkwardness, no polite attempts to shoot the breeze, just a strange, implacable distance. Finally, I stopped trying to draw him out and attempted to assume the same posture. It wasn't easy. If Matt wasn't right there between us brokering the conversation, the awkwardness, on my part at least, was almost overwhelming.

That's what I remembered then about Nick Hutchins—an unnerving self-containment bordering on arrogance. Constance was so reserved in her own way that it was nearly impossible to see how they had ever communicated with each other. But Constance's reserve left the impression of a sun enclosed in a small box, not a limitless void as Nick's did. That was the difference.

"I know," Matt said, as if he could read my mind. "It's hard to imagine, isn't it?"

"They're both certainly attractive, but . . ."

"I could never understand it either, but she was taken with him. I used to watch them. I could see it." Matt now held his pen between his hands as if he were going to snap it in two. "It was a silent point of contention between us."

"Between Constance and you?"

He shook his head. "Between Nick and me. You see, I met her first. She was a very sweet girl—sensitive, gentle, kind. I used to shower her with compliments, but it didn't do any good. She never listened. We used to play a game—a kind of Three Questions. If you could meet three people in the world, any three, who would you want to meet? If you could meet three historical figures? If you could go back and relive three days of your life, what three days would you choose? If you could be the CEO of three Fortune 500 companies, which three would you pick? If you could be the author of three classic works of literature? Painted three famous paintings? Written three rock songs? It was endless. We used to compete to see who could come up with the most creative questions. One day she said, 'If you had to use three adjectives to describe me, what would they be?' This wasn't hard for me. I said, 'Intelligent, sensitive, and naïve.' I would have said beautiful, but I knew she wouldn't have liked that. She was very sensitive about her appearance. She didn't like being taken at face value. Despised it, actually, and looked down on men who admired her without knowing her. I turned the question around then and asked her, 'Which three adjectives would you use to describe me?' She thought about it for a few minutes and then said, 'I would say you are loyal, precise, and tolerant.' Tolerant! That upset me, and when she saw how

much it upset me she tried to switch it to flexible, but I thought
that was worse. You see, she's unfailingly honest, almost to a
fault. I wished I'd never asked her the question. Tolerant. That
bothered me for years. And precise? That was little better. 'What
does that mean?' I asked her. 'It means you do things with care,'
she explained. 'I give you intelligent and sensitive, and you give
me loyal, precise, and tolerant?' I couldn't believe it. 'You said I
was naïve. That's not a compliment,' she pointed out. 'It's not
an insult,' I said. But she insisted that precise and tolerant were
not insults, either. We used to have a lot of conversations like
this."

He looked up at the ceiling again. "I remember sitting on the
bus once that ran through campus. It was crowded, and I was
sitting in the back next to the window as we pulled into West
Campus. I saw Nick standing with his hands in his jean pockets
waiting for someone. He had an expectant look on his face as he
watched everyone piling out. He didn't see me looking out the
window, and the bus was so crowded that I hadn't noticed that
Constance was on it. She must have been sitting up near the
front. I saw her get off and walk over to him. She started talking
to him as if something very curious had just happened to her
and she couldn't wait to tell him. I couldn't hear what she
was saying, but I knew the manner, the expression on her face
when she had discovered some new idea or had an interesting story to tell. Like a child, all her energy went into commu-
nicating what she had to say to the exclusion of everything
and everyone else around her. But he wasn't focused in the least
on what she was saying, and while her words rushed past him
like a cool breeze, he held her arm and leaned over and kissed

her on the cheek and took her books out of her hands. She kept talking as they turned and walked down the quad together. He continued staring at her as if she were beyond his comprehension. It seemed to prefigure their future in some way; maybe that's why I've always remembered it. If she had been more trusting, less naïve . . . if he had been more understanding, smarter."

I studied Matt for a moment as this story from the past wound down. "You are a sentimental man," I said. "I would never have imagined it."

His back stiffened. "If you want to look at it that way."

"I want to look at it that way," I said. "How long did it last?"

"Not long."

"What happened?"

"He wasn't honorable," he repeated.

"What does *that* mean?"

"He didn't fight for her. She loved him, but he didn't see it. He didn't understand it."

"But you were his roommate, his best friend. Couldn't you make him see it?"

He shrugged. "Maybe I could have."

"You never said anything?" I asked. "Nothing?"

I was beginning to wonder now who it was who had not been honorable.

"It didn't take him long to find someone else," he said matter-of-factly.

"And what did she do?" She had obviously not run to Matt.

"She directed her attentions elsewhere."

"To other men?" I asked.

Matt shook his head. "No. That was what was so puzzling. She could have had anyone, but after her freshman year she retreated from the party scene completely, and people resented her for it. It didn't seem right that such an attractive girl should willingly take herself out of circulation, but I suppose she felt it was all a big waste of time. After that first semester, she began funneling all of her energy into her classes. Whenever I went up to the library to our special place behind the Chinese literature section in the stacks, she'd be there poring over her *Norton Anthology of Poetry* or analyzing the narrative techniques of some novelist like Henry James, oblivious to the world. I used to tease her about it, but secretly I respected her. She obviously had a passion for something, which few of us had in those days." He looked at the papers on his desk. "Or still do, for that matter."

"I have something I want to show you," I said. "Just . . . just stay there. I'll be right back."

"This is my office, Morgan," he reminded me. "I'm not going anywhere."

I ran down to my own office and pulled "A Dialogue in Silence" out of my files and went back and set it on his desk. "Have you ever seen this poem?"

He said he hadn't.

"Read it," I said, as I settled back into my chair.

He leaned forward, and I watched his eyes run down the page like an accountant's reviewing a quarterly earnings statement.

"It's beautiful, isn't it?"

He nodded. "She can't get this published?"

"We're trying."

He handed the poem back to me.

"Did you ever tell her how you felt?" I asked.

He looked up at me, surprised.

"It's so obvious," I said. "Please, don't bother denying it."

He studied me for a moment and then sighed heavily. "I did say to her once, 'You know I'm madly in love with you, don't you?' We had just seen *Great Expectations* at a David Lean film festival, and I think the movie had some kind of effect on me. I felt as if I were drunk when I said it, but I wasn't." He began studying his pen again as if he were still trying to piece this out.

"What did she say?"

"She told me I was being ridiculous. 'No, Matt,' she said, 'you are not in love with me.' And that was that. We never discussed it again."

"I see," I said. "Do you know anything about her family or where she came from?"

"She's an only child. Her mother lives in Illinois. Her father was much older than her mother, and he died the year we became friends. I think he had a heart attack. Constance never told me exactly what he died of. She never wanted to talk about it. It was very quick, though, and unexpected."

"That's terrible," I said.

"I know, it was, but she seemed to handle it well. I was with her when her mother called and told her. She showed little emotion. She just packed up her stuff, and I drove her to the airport."

"You must have been a good friend to her," I said.

"I tried."

"Did her family have money?"

"I wouldn't say they had money. They were comfortable. They lived in Lake Forest."

"Illinois?"

"Yes."

I was familiar with Lake Forest. It was one of the wealthiest suburbs on the North Shore.

"Is that where she grew up?"

"One of the places. She went to high school there. Her father worked for some international conglomerate. They moved around a lot."

Matt looked at me then in a way he hadn't looked at me since the days when I used to be his confidante. "Morgan?"

I raised an eyebrow.

"How is she? Did she . . . did she say anything about me?"

I wished I could have said yes, that she'd heaped compliments at his feet and plied me with questions about the state of his marriage, but I couldn't lie. "She seems fine. I don't know really. I don't know her well enough yet. She didn't say anything about you, though, but I think she . . . isn't one to reveal too much of what she's feeling."

"Of course," he said, recovering his managerial demeanor. Lines of anxiety and discomfort were beginning to etch their way onto his face, as if he'd said more than he had intended to say. I tried to put him at his ease.

"Thank you, Matt. I appreciate your honesty. Remember what I said. It doesn't go out of this room. Your secrets are safe with me." I smiled reassuringly. "And thanks, I think she might finally be the writer I've been looking for . . ."

"You're a romantic," Matt declared, as he pulled his chair up to his desk. "You always did want to be Maxwell Perkins."

I smiled. "And you always wanted to be J. P. Morgan."

"I guess you have a better chance of realizing your dream than I do."

I got up from my chair. "I'll keep you posted."

He nodded and went back to his reports.

4

After my conversation with Matt, I went back to my office and sorted through a pile of query letters and book proposals that Linda had left on my desk. Then I put the finishing touches on a pitch I had to deliver to the sales force the following week. I particularly wanted to focus their attention on two books I thought would have great word of mouth if only I could convince them to talk them up a little. One was a historical novel based on the twelfth-century romance of Abélard and Héloise called *A Passion to Resign,* and the other was an epistolary novel in the tradition of *Les Liaisons Dangereuses,* about two late-twentieth-century blue bloods who wreak havoc in the lives of their tightly knit group of friends through their acid-tongued e-mails.

It was a Friday night, and I was supposed to be on a blind date with a friend of my brother's, but I had backed out at the last minute with the most unimaginative of all excuses—a headache. "It's too soon," I told my brother when he called to find out what was going on. My brother was a financial adviser at Morgan Stanley, the only one in the family to break completely away from our academic roots, and he was rather protective of me. "I'm not ready to start over," I told him. When I'd let him set up the date, I was pretty certain that I was ready to venture forth again, but after staring at the photograph of my dead husband on my desk on and off all day, I knew I wasn't. When I could put that photo away, I told him, when I could set it in the back of a drawer in my desk, then I'd know I was ready, but I couldn't do that yet.

I still missed him too much. I missed the late Friday night dinners at our favorite restaurants and the Saturday afternoon walks through Central Park and the simple pleasure of reading *The New York Times* together on a Sunday morning. I was feeling very sentimental about these things; grief does that to people sometimes. The littlest things, the smallest rituals, suddenly take on a significance that they didn't have before. Even the things that used to irritate me had the power now to bring tears to my eyes.

Despite the late hour, I decided to walk home that evening to clear my head. I had so many facts and figures buzzing around in my brain that I thought some air and a little window-shopping would do me good. I set out down Sixth Avenue and turned right on Fifty-fourth Street. It was the middle of October, and I felt a sense of relief that the hot, steamy days of summer were, like a bad memory, safely behind me now. There is nothing quite like Christmas in New York, and I began to look forward to it. I thought about the giant wreaths and big red bows, the toy soldiers, and the tree lights that would all be going up soon. Harbingers of the holiday onslaught.

As I passed the Warwick hotel on my left, a doorman in black pants and a black-and-white-striped vest dashed past me to hail a cab for a departing guest. The hotel's ornate architecture evoked an Old World feeling that made me wish I were on vacation or taking a European tour. As I passed Ciao Europa, the restaurant on the first floor of the hotel, I stopped before the large plate-glass window that framed the diners inside. It was already nine o'clock, and the room was packed with business executives and well-heeled tourists luxuriating in the castlelike setting. I couldn't help envying them. They looked, through my widow's eyes, as if they didn't have a care in the world. They seemed relaxed and at ease with the world. I stared for a moment at the gold-and-brown-toned mural of Queen Isabella of Spain blessing Christopher Columbus's voyage to the New World, and then my eyes scanned the room and came to rest on a couple not more than five feet in front of me.

A distinguished older gentleman in a charcoal-gray suit was sitting with a young woman in a black strapless dress. Her hair was in a neat French twist, and there was a pearl choker around her neck. I couldn't see her face, but the gentleman looked vaguely familiar. I thought perhaps he was someone famous. Graying at the temples, tan, his eyes heavy with the vision in front of him, he seemed to hang on her every word. And yet the way he sat back in his chair and held himself erect, his hand mindlessly fingering the end of the fork on the table in front of him, gave him an air of dignity that could easily, under eyes less used to analyzing character than mine, have been mistaken for indifference. I was about to move away when the woman turned her face slightly to the left, and Constance's unmistakable profile came into focus.

It suddenly seemed important that I not be observed, and I

backed away to avoid drawing attention to myself. But Constance and her dinner companion went right on talking like two characters in a movie. They were stunningly oblivious to the world around them.

Observing them in their public seclusion, I felt like a little girl peering over the banister at a cocktail party. The feeling of being invisible was acute, and in some obscure way, disappointing. A moment or two later, I found my feet again and began walking down Fifty-fourth Street, blind now to the teeming crowds and fancy window displays. I tried to place the man with the graying temples and the tan face and the attentive eyes, but I couldn't quite. I knew he wasn't an actor. He looked like a business executive, but that could be deceptive. Anybody wearing a suit nowadays looked like a business executive. Maybe he was in politics. I racked my brain, but I could not put a name to the tantalizingly familiar face. By the time my mammoth white brick apartment building came into view, I felt almost indignant that Constance hadn't contacted me in the past month, and I made a mental note to call her and find out what she'd been up to lately. For some reason, perhaps a misplaced sense of proprietorship, I felt I had a right to do this.

The following Monday, under a damp, silvery morning fog, I descended the steps of the Lexington Avenue subway line and wedged my way into a car. After the first stop, a seat opened up behind me, and, like a child playing musical chairs with the other straphangers, I quickly sat down. A man in a tattered wool coat, with deep-set eyes and sunken cheeks, was sitting next to me leafing through a copy of the *New York Post*. Out of the corner of my eye, I glanced at pages full of headlines like TOP COP

IN THE SOUP and WHATEVER LILA WANTS . . . My attention, diffuse and unfocused, converged in a flash when he flipped to the *Post's* infamous Page Six. There, in the gossip column, among the movie stars and socialites, was the following:

> Lou Ellis, gentleman CEO of Bartley & Ellis Investments, was seen at Ciao Europa in deep conversation with a mysterious beauty. Who was she? Only Lou can say, and he's not talking. Neither is his wife.

Something in me froze up as a cold light of recognition fell over my mind, and I put the name in the gossip column to the dignified man I had seen Constance dining with Friday night.

Lou Ellis was a partner in one of the most influential venture capital firms on Wall Street. He was known for having an almost unfailing eye for the next big thing. His specialty was technology companies, and he'd ridden the wave of the burgeoning Internet industry like a champion surfer. He had started investing in tech start-ups long before they became fashionable. Consequently, because of his long and illustrious track record, every move he made was carefully monitored and dissected. Lou, though, made a conscious effort to keep his face out of the newspapers and magazines. He rarely gave interviews, never appeared on television, and made the majority of his donations to charity without fanfare, but still, he couldn't keep people from talking about him. His name was inevitably mentioned anytime anyone was talking about creating, buying, or selling a dot-com start-up.

He was also a model philanthropist. It was widely known that he'd funneled a great deal of his wealth back into the community in the form of charitable organizations that he had founded himself. As the squib in the *Post* indicated, his nickname was "the Gentleman"—which was meant to be both descriptive and ironical. He was a transplanted Southerner who'd firmly ensconced himself in the Manhattan social milieu. His manners were impeccable and served to soften the blow when he did business with novices. An expert negotiator, he did not suffer fools gladly. He had no patience for mediocrity and was known to excuse himself quietly and leave the room when he was not happy with what a potential business associate put on the table. His life had also reportedly been touched by tragedy. When he was young, a beloved younger sister had contracted polio and ended up in a wheelchair. Some people thought that this tragedy was part of the reason he was so generous with his money, but nobody really knew for sure.

I pondered the ramifications of a possible relationship between Lou Ellis and Constance. If true, the fact that she had captured such a man's attention was reason for wonder and admiration. How had she met him? Was there really a romantic connection there? And if there was, what did it mean? Lou Ellis was known as a family man. He was also a great proponent of children. He had founded the Society for the Advancement of Youth, SAY, to give children born into poverty a fighting chance to succeed in the world by providing them with computers and training. He had a spotless reputation. I recalled seeing his photograph once in *The New York Times* at a fundraiser at the Plaza hotel—one of the relatively few photos ever published of him—and noting how distinguished and handsome he looked.

When I got to the office, despite having contracts to review and phone calls to make, I began to ruminate. I pulled out the binder of Constance's poems and started to flip through them. Soon enough I was projecting meaning into the lines she had written where perhaps there was none. I read the following poem as if it were some kind of proof of a relationship between the two of them:

INTERIOR DECORATING

Your love for me
Incorporates at least two worlds—
You've decorated your mind with me.
I live within.
Everywhere you look
There is something to remind you about me.
It's in the rose-colored hues that echo my skin;
It's in the blue in the wallpaper
That recalls my eyes and the places I've been.
My hair is captured in the mirror's gold-gilt trim.
There is nothing wrong here,
Nothing to do with sin.
Sometimes love in the outside world
Doesn't fare as well.
Everything becomes more complicated
When a secret is told,
Especially when a simple admirer
Never had any intention of falling.
There are laws to obey.

And I, too, have to remember my artistic calling.
There's no place to hide in this kind of world,
No shade.
My skin would be ruined by the sun's exposure;
My life delayed.
So I look for a third way.
I move to the top of the world
Where everything is white.
The coldness of arctic regions—
Beyond day,
Beyond night.
I pretend that certain things never existed.
I try to think about what's right,
But my heart already knows,
Such transgressions would be alarming.
Pretty soon I wouldn't know which way to go.
I ease myself back into this world
With an understanding of where compromises
     begin,
And the certainty that your love for me
Will never be over.

Time fell away as I read through her work. Before I knew it, the extra hour I had hoped to put in that morning had evaporated. When I heard Linda rummaging through her desk, I shut the binder and resolved to call Constance later that morning. I was thinking about what I wanted to say to her when I looked up and saw Matt standing in the doorway. Thrown off by his appearance—Matt never paid casual visits to my office anymore—I just stared at him. He stepped inside and closed the door.

"What is it?" I asked, alarmed.

He strode over to me and dropped a copy of the *Daily News* on my desk.

"I see you've changed your reading habits," I said in an attempt to diffuse the anxiety coursing through the room. I looked up at him and scrutinized the jagged worry line across his brow. He said nothing but nodded toward the page laid open in front of me. I looked down and my eyes widened. There was a photograph of Constance and Lou Ellis outside of Ciao Europa. They were standing within a little pool of light under the domed awning looking at each other as if they were trying to decide something. The shadowy presence of a man in a black overcoat plunging past them darkened the right side of the photograph.

"I saw them," I said to Matt.

"You saw them?"

"I saw them in the window of Ciao Europa on my way home from work on Friday. I was walking down the street and stopped to look in the window."

"Morgan, did you know that Lou Ellis is on the board of this company?"

"Of Peabody & Simms?"

Matt's eyes searched my office. "Don't you have a copy of the annual report in here?"

"I used to. I might have thrown it out. Linda may have one." I began digging through my desk. "No, here it is." I pulled it from the bottom of a pile of papers. Matt took it from me, opened it up, and stuck it in front of my face, and there he was: Lou Ellis, CEO, Bartley & Ellis Investments, standing with the other board members in front of a ceiling-to-floor bookcase filled with Peabody & Simms titles.

"Wow," I exclaimed.

"Wow. What kind of a response is that? Don't you know the names of the people on the board?"

I shrugged. "I never think about it." The board of directors operated in a rarified atmosphere that felt very remote from my day-to-day editorial activities. It would have been like knowing the names of all the Cabinet members—beside the point.

"You might want to think about it," Matt warned me.

"Okay," I said, and then added, "but why is it so important?"

"Morgan, Lou Ellis and my father are good friends. Constance didn't just come to me out of the blue. My father loves her. We turned her over to you because we wanted an honest evaluation of her work. We knew that was what Constance wanted, too."

I was taking this all in very slowly, as if I were inching my way into a hot bath.

"You know how my father makes it a rule never to interfere with his editors' decisions. He has never broken that rule, and at sixty-seven he's not going to start now. Even for Constance."

I didn't like the fact that Matt had not been completely honest with me about his connection to Constance. He had presented her as a friend from the distant past, but his father's fondness for her implied a much stronger, more immediate attachment. He was so agitated, though, that I decided to let it go. At this point, it didn't really seem to matter.

I shook my head. "But Lou Ellis. How does he fit into this?"

"I don't know. I'm confused about that, too."

"Can you ask your father?"

"He hates gossip, especially about his friends. I don't know."

"They could just be friends," I offered.

He nodded slowly. "They could be."

Our eyes met, and we found there a perfect reflection of each other's doubt and wonder.

5

When I called Constance that afternoon to set up another meeting, I strained to hear something in her voice that might have indicated she was aware of the gossip that was beginning to swirl around her, but I heard nothing. I told her I had to go out of town for a couple of days to a publishing seminar in Boston, but that I wanted to get together with her and see how her work was coming along. We agreed to meet at a midtown restaurant called JUdson Grill at one o'clock the following Friday. It was Monday when I called her, so I had to put this budding story of love and romance on the shelf for a few days and concentrate on the work at hand. This might have been easier to do if I hadn't stuck Constance's binder of poems in my briefcase at the last minute. I found myself paging through them every free moment I got. Poems like the following drew out the philosopher in me and made me curious about her attitude toward God and her religious background. I did not see her as a regular church-goer, though. She was too independent-minded, too original a thinker for that.

LONG BEFORE CHRISTMAS MORNING

Christmas came early this year.
It needed no ribbons or stories.
No presents, no tinsel, no candy canes,
No biblical allegories.
It crept into my heart long before the cold and the
    crowds
And hung there like an ornament on a snow-
    covered bough.
My face shone in the red-tinted, mirrored glass.

I remembered then that I had once been a child.
I remembered I had some questions to ask.

His birth was only the beginning . . .

The Passion of Christ is enacted in the Mass.
He wondered, too, about what had come to pass.
Forsaken, disparaged, humbled, betrayed.

The life of a teacher.
The life of an outcast.

Released from this world,
Was he happy to have his life in the past?
Did he miss the smell of roses?
Did he ever really want to be an iconoclast?

These are the questions I have to ask.
God is sometimes very hard to hear.

Somewhere a woman is posing for a painting.
It helps to have you near.

There was something numinous about those last four lines:

These are the questions I have to ask.
God is sometimes very hard to hear.

Somewhere a woman is posing for a painting.
It helps to have you near.

I found myself going over them again and again, trying to understand what secret or mystery they touched on.

.   .   .

She was punctual this time and walked into the restaurant wearing a close-fitting burgundy skirt with a subtle sheen that caught the light, and a black silk blouse. All of her clothes fit her so precisely that they looked as if they had been made for her. I thought she was fortunate that her slim figure fit the fashions of the times. Her wavy hair was down and tucked behind her ears, and she was holding a small handbag in her right hand. Under her arm was her black leather portfolio. Once again, the host greeted her with a warmth that I thought signaled familiarity.

When she saw me across the elegant steamship of a dining

room, she lifted her head. As she moved toward my table, trailing the host, the ever-present diamond pendant came into view.

"Your skirt is lovely," I said to her as she slipped into her seat. "And your necklace is very beautiful. I was admiring it last time."

She touched the circular pendant. "Thank you very much."

"Is it a family heirloom?"

She indicated it wasn't.

"It's unique." I couldn't stop staring at it. "Did you find it in New York?"

"It was a gift. It's an antique."

"Ah, I can see that now that I really look at it," I told her. "Do you know when it was made?"

"The 1920s, I think."

"The flapper era."

She nodded. "I guess so."

Perhaps, I thought, it was a gift from Lou. It looked like something a man of his distinction might pick out for a woman like Constance.

"It suits you."

"Thank you."

"Would you ladies like something to drink?" We both looked up at a young man with jet-black hair and sparkling white teeth.

"I'd just like some water, please, with a slice of lemon," Constance said.

"Tap or Pellegrino?"

"Tap, please."

"And I'll have an iced tea."

He smiled at us brightly. "I'll be right back with your order."

Constance watched him walk away and then leaned over to me and whispered, "What is wrong with New York tap water? Why would anyone pay eight dollars for a bottle of water? The fact that they ask you . . . it's annoying."

"The water in New York is supposed to be very clean," I conceded, thinking she had a point.

"Exactly."

This little aside about New York City tap water gave me the impression that she felt more comfortable with me now. Emboldened by this flimsy confidence, I began a discussion I hoped would lead to deeper revelations. I knew she didn't trust me enough to reveal anything about her personal life, and she was right to be cautious. But my motives were pure, and I had to find a way to convince her of this if only to make her see that she was risking her reputation and her good name by getting involved with a public figure. It would be one thing to get involved with a man of Lou's stature after she had established herself as a writer, but it was quite another thing to do so before then. People wouldn't understand it. They would label her a home-wrecker, and I had to make her understand this. I cared about her too much now not to.

"So, tell me, how is the writing going?" I asked her.

"I thought of an idea for a novel," she said, "but I'm afraid I haven't made much headway with it. It isn't easy."

"I didn't say it would be easy."

"Yes, I know that. I mean it's different. Writing a novel is very different from writing poetry. It requires a kind of talent I'm not sure that I have."

"Don't say that. You have to believe you can do it."

She glanced out over the room, at the large copper urns filled with evergreen boughs and then up toward the two-story-high ceiling. She seemed to be processing something. To this day, I have never met anyone whose thinking, when she wasn't trying consciously to conceal it, was so visible. You could see each thought move across her face as if it were a seismograph. Everything registered.

"I didn't come here entirely empty-handed. A friend of mine told me to try writing out my idea in poetry, so I brought you what I came up with."

"I'd love to see it."

Constance opened the portfolio she had been holding when she came in and handed me ten or eleven crisp white sheets of paper.

I looked at the title—"The Mutual Muse."

"I wrote some wraparound text," she added hesitantly.

"Do you mind?" I asked, nodding toward the manuscript.

"No, no, of course not," she said, as our waiter returned with our drinks.

I skipped the three-paragraph introduction, which she'd entitled "An Author's Apology," and began to read:

THE MUTUAL MUSE

The actress moves behind the mask
Of the character she plays.
She listens for the voice
In the words she's supposed to say.
The gestures may come naturally

Or be pulled from faraway.
Costumes like the words of a playwright
Fit the style of the day.
The actress envelops herself completely
In this masquerade . . .

The poem told the story of the relationship between an established film director and a young actress. In the poem, Constance explored the idea of being both a muse and a creator at one and the same time, a theme that I later came to understand held a special fascination for her.

It ended on a note of resolution and mutual understanding:

Their loyalties in this film
Had been fused.
They would work together
And together discover things new.
They would be, one for the other,
A mutual muse . . .

Samuel Aberdeen loved Geraldine
Because she let herself be.
Her devotion went beyond him;
It was mixed up with the sea.
He loved her partly for her beauty
But mostly for what in her was unseen.
Her soul like a tree grew within her
Both leafy and green.

I looked up at her. "Do you know what this poem proves?" I asked her.

"What?"

"It proves that you can tell a story."

She thought about this for a moment, turning it over carefully in her mind. I remained silent, letting the idea sprout roots and take hold in her imagination. "I have a confession to make," she finally said.

"Yes."

"I've always wanted to write a novel. I've just had a terrible block about it for so long that I didn't want to tell you. I don't like disappointing people."

Her sensitivity to my feelings was touching, if misplaced. "Please don't worry about disappointing me, Constance. It's very hard to be a novelist if you're worried about disappointing people. Writing is difficult enough as it is. You just have to work and do the best you can." The last thing I wanted was for her to feel anxious. If she envisioned me peering over her shoulder every time she sat down to write, she'd never get anywhere.

"You have a very wise friend," I told her.

She looked at me.

"The friend who told you to write your idea out in poetry. That was an excellent idea. I should have recommended it myself."

"Yes," she said, brightening. "He's very smart."

"Is he a writer, too?"

"No."

"Is he in publishing?"

"No. He's kind of a teacher."

"A writing teacher?"

"Not exactly."

"It's good to have friends like that who can help you," I said.

"Yes, he helps me a great deal."

"I was just talking with Matt this morning about a very intelligent man who is on the board of Peabody & Simms."

The hopeful expression on her face began to fade.

"Lou Ellis. Have you ever heard of him?"

At the mention of his name, her face became a mask of perfect calm. The seismograph had been abruptly turned off. She continued to stare at me, and when I asked her if she'd heard of him, she said simply, "Of course."

"Which part of the poem did you like the best?" she asked.

I looked her in the eye. At this point our waiter, who had been hovering in the background, approached and asked if we were ready to order. I don't remember what either one of us chose. I do remember that Constance told the waiter what she wanted with the gravity of a prisoner on death row ordering her last meal. As soon as he retreated, I closed in on her.

"Constance, do you ever read the *New York Post* or the *Daily News*?"

She shook her head.

"I didn't think so. I came across copies of both of these newspapers earlier this week, and Lou Ellis figured prominently in the gossip columns. Apparently, he has been seen out on the town with a mysterious young woman."

Her unblinking, sphinxlike focus on what I was saying was impossible to read. I had no idea whether I was offending her or getting through to her.

"I was walking home from work last Friday and saw the two of you in the window of Ciao Europa. I recognized you, of course, but not the man you were with until I spotted his name in the *Post*. There was a photograph of the two of you outside the restaurant in the *Daily News* on Monday."

She flinched this time as if somewhere deep within her I had just touched, with an icy finger, the softest, most vulnerable region of her heart. She recovered quickly, though.

"I know it might seem like I'm being intrusive," I added calmly, "but I honestly want to be helpful. I think you should know that you are risking your own professional future by getting involved with a married man like Lou Ellis. You haven't established yourself yet. No one knows anything about you, so they can make you out to be whatever they want you to be—gold digger, mistress, gal pal. Now, if he were divorced or if you were established that would be another thing, but that is not the way it is, and you need to see that."

The words coming so forcefully out of my mouth were not the words I had planned on saying. There was something about her aloof, impenetrable nature, though, that made me feel extraordinarily protective. Like a lawyer trying to defend an uncooperative client, I was anxious for my arguments to make an impression.

She was observing me now as if I were a puzzle she was trying to solve. Her brow had tightened and her eyes had narrowed. As our salads were set before us, she put her napkin in her lap and took a sip of water.

"Thank you for your advice, Morgan. I appreciate your concern. Now, I believe you wanted to talk to me about my writing.

Do you think the story I told in the poem could be expanded into a novel?"

And so for the rest of our lunch, now that she had put me firmly in my place, we discussed the technical difficulties involved in writing a novel: plot, story development, pacing, conflict, voice, and that ever-elusive thing called style.

I was impressed with her single-mindedness and her attention to detail. She said she'd been studying *The Great Gatsby.* "I've read it three times in the last two months." And she tried to explain to me what she had taken from it. "It's ironic that in portraying the lives of a bunch of Long Island socialites and their various love affairs, Fitzgerald got at something extremely profound. It took me a while to see it, but now that I do, it's stunning. I don't think you can fully appreciate that book, though, until you have a certain amount of life experience to draw from. Otherwise it can seem a fairly trivial story, but it would be a mistake to think that. And the fact that the book defined the Jazz Age is a small matter compared with the psychology in that novel."

"And what do you mean exactly by the psychology in the novel?"

"It has to do with the love Gatsby feels for Daisy. It goes far beyond the normal love of a man for a woman," she said, determined, I could tell, to ignore the frustration in my voice. "It's much bigger, and at the same time, much smaller—smaller because it really has little to do with her as a person. Bigger because it encompasses every dream he has ever had for himself. She's a symbol—a symbol of success, wealth, love, happiness, romance, and inclusion. It's a projected love that is extremely seductive and powerful, and it is the hardest kind of love to endure whether you are giving or receiving it. And sometimes when you have loved someone from a distance, and you finally get up close to them, the way Gatsby did with Daisy, you find that the symbol begins to disintegrate before your eyes, or it detaches itself from the person and lives in your imagination, where, if you're lucky, you might be able to deal with it. Gatsby wasn't lucky."

"No," I said. "I guess he wasn't."

"I've been thinking a lot about Fitzgerald," she continued, unfazed by my tepid response. "I found the most amazing book in the Gotham Book Mart a few weeks ago. It's a pictorial autobiography from the scrapbooks of Fitzgerald and his wife, Zelda. It was put together by their daughter, Scottie. It's the most wonderful book, full of primary sources—newspaper clippings, photographs, book reviews, even theater stubs and little penciled notes. Fitzgerald was a meticulous record keeper, and it gives a much truer sense of the time than anything else I've read, except *The Great Gatsby*, of course. If you really want to understand what it was like to live during a particular era, it is always better to go back to primary sources, to novels and books published during the period you're studying, rather than to historical accounts written years after the fact. I learned that from one of my history professors in college. Distortion, he used to say, always sets in as soon as something is over."

I nodded, softening somewhat in the face of her resolve.

"I always try to keep that in mind," she said pensively.

And so that was how the conversation went. After discussing the parallels between Fitzgerald's life story and the themes and characters in *The Great Gatsby,* we talked at length about the importance of thoroughly transforming your experiences when writing a novel and how successful Fitzgerald had been at doing this.

"It probably doesn't occur to most readers that there was a life behind this book," I remember her saying. "He didn't just invent the story out of thin air. There was twenty-nine years of experience in that book."

By the time we had finished lunch and were standing in the atrium of the Equitable Building just outside the restaurant, she seemed fairly at ease. The personal business at the beginning of lunch, apparently, in her mind, now completely forgotten. But I hadn't forgotten it. Before she left, I made one more attempt. "Just remember, Constance, if you ever need a friend, I'll be your friend."

I saw a sadness fall over her face then that reminded me of sunsets and good-byes and all things final. Her eyes, heavy with the weight of her secrets, seemed to want to tell me something. She reached out her hand. "Thank you for lunch, Morgan. It was kind of you to invite me."

"Work hard," I said.

"I will," she assured me, and hurried away.

6

Three days after our meeting, I received a note from Constance thanking me for a "thought-provoking lunch." Included with the card was a folded sheet of paper with the following poem printed on it:

THE PRIVACY OF METAPHORS

Something divides me.
It's all the secrets
I've never told—
The memories inside me
That are starting to grow old.
Listening to the intimate lives of strangers
Makes me lose my breath.
Even within a novel,
I feel this kind of death.
I prefer metaphors
And the security of quiet rooms.
Telling everything
Was never something I meant to do.

Love found me and held me in its embrace;
A city rose up over the horizon;
People began to recognize my face.
But I said nothing,
As if I'd never been to that place.

I think, paradoxically, it was Constance's reticence that drew me to her the most. There was something very touching and old-fashioned about having secrets and guarding them so devotedly. Trying to understand her gave me a certain amount of pleasure, mainly because she was so different from everybody else I knew. The absence of concrete facts about her life gave me the opportunity to weave my own story out of the few bits and pieces that I could fit together. She seemed, like my historical novelist's Héloise, a decidedly romantic figure.

It was with surprise, therefore, and a certain amount of alarm, that I received a phone call from her roughly three weeks after our lunch meeting. I remember it was two o'clock in the afternoon because I was about to go into a meeting with Matt, and I ended up being ten minutes late. He was mollified and curious, though, when I explained that I had had an unexpected call from Constance. Her voice was tremulous and the words came haltingly, but her message was clear. Something disturbing had happened, and she wanted to speak to me about it—that evening, if possible.

I told her I thought I could get out of the office by five o'clock and agreed to meet her in the Cocktail Terrace of the Waldorf-Astoria. She said we could get a drink there and talk privately.

I knew this time, of course, not to confront her directly. I would wait, and I would watch, and I would listen. She was already sitting at a low table next to the balcony with a glass of water in front of her when I arrived. Dressed in a black cashmere turtleneck, a long narrow charcoal-gray skirt, and black boots, she looked the epitome of New York chic. Her blue eyes were busy with life, and her face was flushed and burning with dammed-up emotions. Despite all this, she stood and greeted me in her usual formal manner and thanked me politely for coming.

"I know it was all very last minute, and I'm sorry for that," she apologized.

I told her not to worry about it. "I said I wanted to be your friend, and friends are always on call."

She smiled and we sat down. People were walking back and forth across the pastel Wheel of Life mosaic in the center of the lobby floor. Some were talking and laughing, briefcases or shopping bags in hand, others moved about in determined silence. Except for a young man in a gray pullover and black trousers sitting in the corner reading a magazine and a piano player spinning out sentimental love songs on a grand piano at the other end of the lounge, we were, for all intents and purposes, alone.

Constance clasped her hands together in her lap and lowered her chin. "I have to confess," she began, "that I have never really had a close girlfriend or anyone to confide in . . . in that way that women do sometimes. I have always felt that a strong person should be able to deal with her problems by herself."

"I can understand that, but sometimes it does help to have someone to talk to, don't you think?"

"Yes," she said, eyeing me warily. "I think you're right."

I reached out my hand and touched her arm. "When I said I wanted to be your friend, Constance, I meant it."

This reassurance seemed to put her at ease, and she unclasped her hands.

"It's hard to know where to begin," she said. "I just know I need to talk to someone. Someone who can be objective."

"I'll do the best I can."

"I'm coming to you because of the things you said at lunch. You were right. You did see me having dinner with Lou at Ciao Europa. I was shocked when you brought it up because our relationship has been a very . . . ," her eyes wandered as if she were waiting for someone to tell her how to proceed, "private one. I've never discussed it with anyone before, and now it's in the newspapers, or, I should say, *tabloids*." Disgust seeped into her voice at the enunciation of the loathsome word.

"So you saw the newspapers?"

"Yes, Lou showed them to me. He's rather upset about it."

"But he's a smart man. He must have known he might be recognized when he was with you."

She shrugged. "We've been going out to dinner together for two years, and nothing like this has ever happened."

"Maybe you just got complacent. You were sitting in the window seat, after all."

"I know, but"—she stopped herself and gave me the once-over again—"I have my suspicions."

"Suspicions?"

She sighed heavily and stared intently across the room at the piano. For a moment, I thought she was going to tell me she had changed her mind and she had to leave, but, after compassing the room one more time with her eyes, she continued. "It's a long story."

"I'm not in a hurry." As soon as these words passed through my lips, I realized that it had been a long time since I had expressed sentiments such as these. I was always in a hurry.

"All right, then," she said. "But please give me your word of honor that this is between you and me and no one else. I need to be able to trust somebody."

"You can trust me."

"Yes, I think I can." She looked at me then as if by a mere glance she could take the full measure of my soul. "I guess the first thing I need to tell you is that Lou and I met almost seven years ago when I was getting my MBA at Columbia."

"You have an MBA?" This didn't fit at all with the romantic picture of her I had created in my imagination.

"Yes, but it isn't something I like to talk about. My father wanted me to go to business school so I'd always have something to fall back on if the writing didn't work out. He died when I was an undergraduate, and before he passed away he made me promise that I would get it and I did. He was my sole motivation. It would have been a complete wash except for Lou. He was a professor at Columbia then. This was a few years before he founded Bartley & Ellis Investments."

"He was a professor?" I said, surprised. It seemed like something I should have known.

"Yes, and a very good one. I took two classes with him. One was a course on managing innovation and the other was an elective course on the history of technology—one of the most exciting classes I've ever taken. He opened my mind up to the difference between discovery and invention and taught me to weigh the economic, political, military, and social factors that prompt new developments. Now, whenever I think about the impact of a new technology, I examine it from all these viewpoints. I see the world differently because of him. He taught me how to take in the big picture, which is very important for a writer."

"Yes, it is," I said. "Vitally important."

"Anyway, I was, by his admission, one of his best students. I asked a lot of questions—he could always count on me to get a class discussion going—and I guess I was pretty enthusiastic. His class was just so much more interesting than the rest of my classes. He told me later that he admired me, but I didn't know that then."

"I see," I said. "So he never showed any overt interest in you when you were a student."

"Definitely not," Constance said. "He was very proper in that respect. I graduated, said good-bye, and that was that. I never expected to see him again. Then, about five years after graduation, I was walking home from work one evening, staring absently at the merchandise in the shop windows, thinking about my father's death—he died just before Christmas—when this feeling suddenly came over me that something was going on that night at the 92nd Street Y that I wouldn't want to miss. I hate missing things, and I especially hate discovering after the fact that someone I would really like to have seen, like William Styron or Joyce Carol Oates, was being interviewed somewhere and I missed it. It was a couple of weeks before Christmas, and this feeling just blew over me like the north wind. So I walked up to Ninety-second Street and went into the Y to see what was going on. A young man behind the ticket counter said, 'Lou Ellis of Bartley & Ellis is speaking tonight on the impact of the Internet.' 'Lou Ellis,' I said. 'The professor from Columbia?' He picked up the fall-winter brochure and looked up his bio. 'The same man,' he said."

"That must have shocked you." Her willingness to follow an impulse through to its logical conclusion only heightened for me that otherworldly aspect of her I'd already found so intriguing.

"It did," she said. "I pulled twenty dollars out of my purse and bought a ticket. As I said, Lou had been a special professor for me at Columbia, and the prospect of seeing him again had a certain charm to it. It seemed a wonderful act of fate, a kind of early Christmas present, and I remember feeling my mood lighten. I stood in front of the auditorium for an hour so I could get a good seat when they opened the doors.

"When he came out, after a very flattering introduction by the program coordinator, I noticed that he had aged hardly at all and was still quite handsome, but he looked weary, as if he'd walked ten miles to get there. Once he began talking, though, and outlining the social, political, and economic ramifications of the information revolution, his eyes brightened, and the whole auditorium was charged with a wonderful feeling of enthusiasm. People were literally sitting on the edge of their seats as he spoke. Afterward, during the Q&A, he was barraged with questions. I had the sense that a lot of day traders were in the audience who wanted to get a handle on where the market was going. My question—because, of course, I had to ask a question—had nothing to do with the stock market."

"What did you ask him?" I said.

"I raised my hand and said, 'Professor Ellis, the Internet allows us to transfer messages and documents to each other in
seconds, but the telegraph also dramatically reduced the time it
took to send information to someone—from days and weeks,
sometimes months, to minutes. Could you please talk about
the impact of Morse's invention of the telegraph in the mid-
1800s versus the impact of the Internet today? Didn't the telegraph force the same level of adjustment?' Something like that.
My question made him smile, *one,* because he recognized me—
I was sitting in the second row—and *two,* because it was straight
from one of his classes. We had talked at length in his class at
Columbia about the ramifications of the invention of the telegraph in the middle of the nineteenth century. So, that night at
the Y, he made a compelling argument in favor of the Internet's
greater impact. But, he also used my question to make a case
with the audience that the Internet was not something to be
afraid of, because throughout history, and in particular the last
two hundred years, people have had to adapt to a great many
technological innovations and have done so with amazing ease.
And then he told an amusing little story about the telephone
and how people couldn't imagine at first what purpose it would
serve. 'If I had one, who in the world would I call?' People used
to ask questions like that, he said. They looked at it as a novelty,
not as an exciting new communications tool.

"There was thunderous applause at the end, and as it died
down, he looked out over the packed house. Then he nodded
deferentially in my direction and walked off the stage. The program coordinator came out, thanked him profusely for being
there, and invited everyone to a reception in the lounge next

door. I sat there for a few minutes while everyone piled out around me. The respectful, courteous expression on his face when he looked at me kept running through my head, and I found myself filled with a feeling of awe and wonder. Wonder that he had noticed me, and wonder that he wanted me to *know* that he had noticed me. There was something about the look in his eyes when he nodded at me that gave me the feeling of being clearly singled out, which was a very powerful sensation in that packed auditorium."

"It must have been," I said.

"It was," she said. "I was preparing to go in to the reception next door when I caught sight of Lou in the little hallway that runs from the back of the stage to the lounge. He saw me and hesitated. I stood up. He stepped out of the crowd into the now nearly empty auditorium."

.   .   .

"My all-time favorite student," he said, reaching out his hand to greet me.

I walked over to him.

"Professor Ellis," I said, "it's so good to see you."

He held my shoulders then and studied me for a few moments as if he were trying to make sure it was really Constance Chamberlain and not someone who merely looked like her.

"You were in top form tonight," I told him.

"It was a good audience."

"A tough one," I said. "You always get a bunch of inquisitors in New York City."

He laughed. "That's what's so wonderful about New York."

He continued to study me. Then his eyes narrowed. "So I see you decided to stay?"

I didn't understand what he meant at first, but then he added, "You didn't go back to Illinois."

"No," I said, surprised that he remembered that I had been thinking about going back.

"And how are things at Goldman Sachs?" I'd begun working at Goldman Sachs after I graduated from Columbia. Lou had been one of my references.

"I'm not at Goldman Sachs anymore," I told him. "I've been working in a bookstore."

"Really?" he said, trying not to look too surprised.

"The Gotham Book Mart on West Forty-seventh Street. Have you heard of it?"

"A bookstore, Constance. No, I'm sorry, I don't think I have."

"Yes," I said proudly. "I'm putting my MBA to good use. I'm working in a bookstore that doesn't stock a single business title."

"And what happened to your job at Goldman Sachs?" he asked. I'd been working in the investment banking division.

"Two years was enough," I said, then leaned over and whispered, "I never told you this, but I never actually had any interest in business. I liked learning about it from you, but I discovered I absolutely do not like being part of it."

"Well, you could have fooled me. You were an excellent student."

I thanked him, then I asked him about his company, Bartleby & Ellis Investments.

"*Bartley* & Ellis Investments," he politely corrected me.

"I'm sorry." I could feel my face turning red. "Bartley & Ellis Investments."

"I guess you've been reading too much Melville."

"I guess maybe I have." And it was true, the night before I had been rereading Melville's "Bartleby, the Scrivener." "I have to confess. I haven't been reading the business pages lately."

He laughed. "That's okay. They're usually pretty boring. It's only in the doing that it is really interesting."

"I remember you used to say that," I said.

At this point, the program coordinator came in and, with a certain amount of hand-wringing, informed Lou that there were a lot of people waiting for him in the next room. "I think you're supposed to be mingling, Professor Ellis," I said.

He told me to call him Lou.

"Lou," I said with some difficulty. The lonely syllable felt very strange on my tongue after all those years of knowing and thinking about him only as Professor Ellis.

"It was wonderful to see you again, Constance," he said, and kissed me on the cheek. Then, after studying my face again for a few moments, he left. I watched him disappear with the program coordinator through the little hallway.

·   ·   ·

"This might sound unbelievable, Morgan, but I really had no notion until that night of the magnitude of his influence—even after that evening, the sheer scope of it simply eluded me. I had immersed myself in my writing so completely that I had never even heard of Bartley & Ellis Investments. When I left Goldman Sachs, I was so tired of analyzing everything in terms of cash flow analysis and balance sheet projections that I just closed my mind to that whole arena. I never read *The Wall Street Journal* or *Business Week* or *Barron's* or even the business section of the *Times*. I reflexively screened out anything that reminded me of those—in my mind—wasted years. I had to make up for lost time at that point, and I threw myself into my writing again. My father had left me a little money, and I had some money I'd saved from Goldman Sachs, so I took the job at the Gotham Book Mart and rented a tiny studio apartment up in the East Nineties. I needed a strictly nine-to-five job with no demands. The rest of my time I spent reading and studying. It was a wonderful period of my life—even, I would say, a romantic period. I had the privilege of being alone with my thoughts and the time to see where those thoughts and ideas might lead me—if I dared to follow them."

"That was a brave thing to do," I told her. "Not many people nowadays would be able to do that."

She considered this for a moment. "It wasn't hard," she said. "I knew if I didn't get back to my writing soon I'd regret it for the rest of my life, and regret is something I'm very afraid of. I never want to have that in my life." She spoke about regret as if it were a nasty, virulent form of mold or some kind of insidious virus.

"I know, but it's hard to avoid sometimes," I said. "Everyone has to make choices."

"That's true, but if you really know what you want out of life, then you can make the right choices without regrets. At least, that's how I see it. Whenever I have a difficult choice to make, I imagine myself on my deathbed looking back over my life, thinking about all the things I did and didn't do. I know there are certain things I could accept having missed. For example, if I never had children, that would be okay. If I never got married, I could accept that, too. But if I had to die knowing that I never became the writer I wanted to be . . . that would be devastating. That would kill me. When I look at things in this way, it helps me determine what's really important to me."

Her clear-eyed devotion was impressive.

"The most important thing is my writing. Anything else that comes along is extra."

"Like Lou," I said.

She hesitated. "No, not exactly." And then she added, sotto voce, "I can't imagine my life without Lou."

"Because you love him?"

"Yes, and because he's helped me so much with my writing. I owe him a great deal." She laughed. "He always says to me that he's number two. The writing is number one, and he's number two, but that isn't true. I don't rank them."

"But that's what he thinks."

"Yes, that's what he thinks, sometimes. When I can't convince him otherwise." She stopped for a moment to think about this. Then she glanced around the room as if she were seeing it with new eyes and, after taking a sip of her water, returned to her story. "It was four or five days after our meeting at the Y that Lou surprised me by showing up at the Gotham Book Mart. I was sorting through the new poetry books and restocking the shelves, when I overheard Stan, the cashier at the front of the store, say, 'She's right there.' I looked up and saw Lou, dressed in a custom-tailored suit. I wanted to smile because he looked so out of place in that antiquated, slow-paced shop, but the intense look in his eyes forced all expression from my face. I just stood there and watched him move toward me."

I stared in fascination then as Constance mentally took herself back to that afternoon at the Gotham. Their conversation flowed from her virtually intact. She apparently remembered everything—from Lou's first question to his last. And Lou's first question was obvious enough. "He asked me if I could help him find a book," Constance said. "I asked him what he was looking for."

.   .   .

"A copy of Alexis de Tocqueville's *Democracy in America,*" he told me. The tension in his voice, Morgan, was so pronounced that I could feel my own composure threatening to shatter into a thousand pieces.

"We don't have a large history section," I managed to get out, "but I can check."

I went and searched through the history books and looked in the storage rooms upstairs but couldn't find anything. "I'm sorry," I said when I came back. "We usually carry it, but we don't have it right now. I could get it for you, though."

"That's all right," he said.

"You could probably order it online on that website— Amazon," I suggested. "Supposedly, they can get you anything you want. Of course, I shouldn't be recommending them, but if you need it in a hurry, I think they'll send it overnight."

"Thank you, Constance," Lou said. "That's fine. I have to be going now."

And he left. I remember standing there in a daze, watching him pass by the front window. I couldn't imagine what a man of his stature would be doing in the Gotham Book Mart in the middle of the afternoon. If he were really in need of a copy of *Democracy in America*, he certainly did not need to go out and dig it up himself. He could send an assistant to do that or just call the store and have it delivered. But he hadn't done that. He'd come into the store, and he had specifically asked for me. It seemed very peculiar, almost unbelievable. But there it was. And then he came back again the next day. This time he said he was looking for a copy of Thoreau's *Civil Disobedience*. Fortunately, we had it in stock. I handed it to him with a little flourish and asked him if he was writing an article. He said no. I asked him if he was preparing a speech. Again he said no.

"I'm just doing a little independent studying," he told me.

"Really? Do you like to do that? To study things on your own?" I was thrilled at the idea of talking to someone who approached learning the same way I did.

"Yes," he said. "I've always been an independent scholar."

"That's what I am," I told him.

"It's one of the best things you can be," he said.

I agreed. "I latch on to subjects or people and want to learn everything I can about them. Most of the time an artist will capture my imagination or a particular painting or a book. I like studying psychology, too, and history. Science, a little less so. I don't have the background. I just finished a run through the collected works of Carl Jung. It took me six months, and I had to read certain things over and over again before I really understood them, but it was fascinating. It was actually one of the most exciting periods of my life, reading his books. He's one of those people who put you in touch with the things that are right in front of you that you can't see. Before that I was all wrapped up in Emily Dickinson. I ordered every obscure book on her that I could—"

"Constance," he said, reaching out and grabbing my hand. "I'd really love to hear all about this. Please, go to dinner with me tonight. I have a meeting this evening, but I'll be done by seven."

I stared at him for a few seconds as if he'd just invited me to the moon. "Yes," I finally got out. "That would be nice."

"All right, then. I'll meet you at La Réserve. It's in the middle of Rockefeller Center on Forty-ninth Street, across from the skating rink."

I repeated the name of the restaurant so I wouldn't forget it.

He smiled at me like a little boy on Christmas morning; then he tipped his hat and left the store. I remember watching his back as he moved away from me toward the door, and it seemed to me as if he were leaving a trail of fairy dust in his wake that momentarily transformed this dusty little bookshop into something infinitely magical and mysterious. I'll never forget it.

7

Constance was looking off into space now as if she had just entered a world of diamonds and perfume. Then she sighed deeply. "So that's how it began, in the back of the Gotham Book Mart, on a cloudy Wednesday afternoon, in the middle of December. Not exactly the spot you would pick for the inception of a grand romance."

"Is it a grand romance?" I asked.

She smiled. "To me it is."

"And to him?"

"It definitely is." She looked over the terrace balustrade. I followed her gaze and saw a couple—newlyweds, perhaps—walking hand in hand through the hotel lobby. "So we had our first dinner together at La Réserve. At that time in my life I was economizing on everything, from the food I ate to the clothes I bought. I walked everywhere or took the subway and never set foot in a cab. So an evening out at a restaurant like La Réserve was something quite special, something I'd never experienced before, and I remember feeling a bit awkward. It was as if I had stepped into a fairy tale. There were no prices on the menu and the salad was served *after* the meal. It was all very strange to me, but Lou was perfectly at home there. 'This is the perfect setting for a woman like you,' he said. He treated me as if I were a princess, and when he looked into my eyes, which he did a lot that evening, I could tell that something was going on within him that was a little beyond me. We talked about everything from the most promising Internet start-ups to the ballets of George Balanchine. He had something interesting to say about every subject, even subjects that were new to him. I felt as if I could have talked to him for days without the slightest lull in the conversation, and this simple fact was a revelation for me. It thrilled me no end because it was something new. In the past, when I would go out with a man, I often had the feeling that I was listening to myself talk. I could never explain it exactly, but it always made me pull back. I used to ask myself if there was something wrong with me. It never occurred to me that it might not be me, that it was *them*. The fact that I could carry on a conversation with a man of Lou's stature made me look at myself differently. 'Aha,' I thought. 'Maybe this has been my problem. Maybe I just needed someone more stimulating. Maybe, just maybe,' I thought for the first time in my life, 'all those other men bored me.' "

She laughed. "That might sound strange, but you only know what you know. If you haven't experienced what it's like to have a real give-and-take in a conversation, you simply don't know that it's possible. I will always have Lou to thank for showing me that it is possible."

It struck me as she said this that there must be a certain loneliness that comes with being, intellectually at least, beyond your peers. It seemed odd that it would take her encounter with Lou for this to become apparent to her, but then she didn't seem like someone who was inclined to locate the reasons for her problems outside of herself. This was in some ways a noble characteristic, but also a dangerous one. As her story developed, I began to see that time and time again it had led her astray, without her ever being the least bit aware of it. It was the kind of characteristic in someone of Constance's age and temperament that could lead to all sort of doubts and self-recriminations.

"Before he put me in a cab that night, I looked at him. 'I have to give you a hug,' I said. We embraced and he whispered to me, 'You're a sweetheart. You know that, don't you?' And as the cab pulled away and I turned to wave to him out the back window, I realized that I was about to fall in love with this man. I knew this because I was missing him before he had even said good-bye. I could already feel the lack of his presence. I'd never gone out with anyone who made me feel that way before. I wasn't even aware that that kind of longing was possible, until that moment."

"So Lou was your first love?" I said.

"Yes, my first love. My first real love." She lingered over the words. "He was a fascinating man. As I said earlier, I knew nothing of his background beyond the fact that he had once been a professor at Columbia and was now the CEO of Bartley & Ellis Investments. When he'd asked me to dinner, I hadn't been sure where he was coming from, and I never assume what I don't absolutely know. It wasn't impossible—unlikely, maybe, but not impossible—that he simply wanted to catch up with an old student who had also been a particular favorite. As much as he en-

joyed building up his business, I could tell he missed teaching. I
thought he was also curious about what I was doing and wanted
to know why I was working in a bookstore. When I told him I'd
been writing, he became intrigued and said he hoped I might
show him some of my work one day. I said I might. A week later
we went to dinner again, and I brought some of my poems with
me. He read each one of them carefully and asked me a lot of
questions about what they meant and how and why I had done
this or that. 'These are *really* good, Constance,' he said. 'These
should be published. You have a great facility with the language.' I thanked him, and he said it again, as if I needed con-
vincing."

"But you didn't," I said to her.

She smiled modestly. "No, I didn't, not at that point. I'm not
the most confident person in the world, but I know a few things
about myself. And one of those things is that I can write. Not
everything I write is fantastic, of course, and a lot of it ends up
in the garbage, but I do get stuff occasionally that stands up."

"Like 'A Dialogue in Silence.' "

"Yes, like that poem. That one has stood up quite well. And
I do reread my poems without cringing. That has to mean
something."

"You know, Constance," I said, "E. B. White wrote, 'All poets
who, when reading from their own works, experience a choked
feeling, are major.' In fact, he said, 'All poets who read from their
own works are major, whether they choke or not.' "

A faint pink glow suffused her high cheekbones. "I don't
know about that," she said, "but I do seem to get something out
of my poems when I go back to them. I learn things."

"I do, too," I said.

She smiled again as if my response pleased her, then she looked once more around the sparsely populated cocktail lounge. "Now, where . . ."

"You were talking about your dinner with Lou."

"Right . . ." Her eyes rested for a moment on something behind me. "At the end of the meal, when we were having our coffee, he became very serious. 'I have a confession to make,' he told me. 'I've been thinking about you more than I should be.' I looked at him. It was the first time anyone had ever spoken to me like that, directly, and I was impressed—taken aback, too—but determined to meet him halfway. 'I don't want to make you uncomfortable,' he added, 'but I'm sure you can pick up how I'm feeling, and it doesn't seem fair to pretend.' We just stared at each other for a few moments, then I said, 'If anyone has a right to think about me, it's you.' I knew somehow that Lou appreciated me in a way that no man had ever appreciated me before. Even my father had never understood my writing or my love for literature or really anything about me. 'Poetry. Novels. Literature. Where is the future in it?' my father used to ask me over and over again. I simply didn't make any sense to him. Nothing I did was practical. But Lou valued the very things about me that my father had dismissed. He saw something in me that I very much wanted to see but never had been able to see before in its entirety, and I think I felt that if I could get closer to him, I could get closer to whatever it was in me that attracted him. It was at this point, before anything had actually happened, but after many invisible lines had been crossed, that I found out I was in trouble. Lou told me he was married. It wasn't a surprise.

I had seen the wedding ring on his finger, but the articulation of the fact did make it real in a way that it hadn't been before. He said it almost apologetically, as if he desperately wished that it weren't true. I wasn't being naïve about this. He meant it. Lou is a shrewd businessman, maybe the shrewdest, but I have in my heart what Hemingway used to call a 'built-in, shock-proof shit-detector,' and I know how to use it. As a writer, you learn to read people. If someone isn't trustworthy, I know. I can't always tell you why or give you specific reasons; I just feel it and the walls go up."

Constance stopped speaking and fixed her eyes on something behind me again. A moment later a waiter came up and asked if he could get us something to drink. We both ordered white wine. As soon as he was out of hearing range, she resumed her story.

"Maybe I should have been more cautious, but once you're in love with someone it isn't possible to stop loving them. Of course, you can avoid seeing them, but I wasn't strong enough to do this. We both tried, but it was impossible. We were drawn to each other as if our whole lives had been leading up to this relationship. Everything else paled dramatically in comparison— marriage, conventional morality, duty, responsibility. They all took a backseat. It was as if a higher morality or set of laws had been set in motion by our efforts to find the truth in our own lives, and I think we both knew that the only way to this truth was through each other. Consequently, anything predicated primarily on obligation and guilt carried little weight, at least for a while."

She sat silent for a moment, then like flashlights trained on the back of an ancient cave, her eyes fell on me again. "Have you ever lived with a secret, Morgan?"

"What do you mean?"

"Have you ever had to pretend that you were someone you're not?"

"No, I don't think so."

"Lou has. He's kept secrets for years that he should never have had to keep. He's kept them faithfully in order to preserve the appearance of normalcy. Keeping a secret requires a lot of energy, and when Lou met me, he was tired. His secrets were weighing him down. He needed, in the most basic way, someone to talk to. That's really how our relationship began. We just started talking."

She lowered her head and clasped her hands together again. Then she looked up at me. "Lou's personal life is very complicated."

"What do you mean, complicated?"

She paused for a moment as if she were trying to decide the best way to approach her subject. "I have to go back in time a way for this to make sense," she said, "so . . ." She looked up then and watched as our waiter set our glasses of wine in front of us. "Thank you," she said as he moved away. She took a sip. "As I said, I have to go back to the beginning in order for you to understand where we are now, so, please, bear with me."

I told her to go back as far as she had to.

"Lou was born in Mississippi," she said, "but he grew up in New Bedford, Massachusetts. He is the oldest of six children. His parents were Catholics and, out of respect for the church, never used birth control. Lou was the only one of the six siblings to really make something of himself. The rest of them were never able to rise above their humble beginnings, and they have all had very hard lives. Lou, though, was the valedictorian of his class and the captain of the football team. He was the proverbial golden boy, and he realized very early that the only way out of his working-class background was through education. He received a scholarship to Yale and was one of only five people in his high school class to go to college. He had no intention of spending the rest of his life in New Bedford scraping by in his father's radio and television repair shop. Like George Bailey in *It's a Wonderful Life,* whom I once teasingly compared him to, he wanted to 'see the world.' So he went off to Yale after graduation and had a spectacular first year—dean's list, treasurer of his class, MVP of the freshman football team. The golden boy was becoming a distinguished young gentleman, and a promising future was opening up before him, filled with opportunity and excitement. All he had to do was walk through the palace gates."

"But, of course, he didn't," I said. My mind was already busy mapping out numerous tragic but familiar story lines.

Constance shook her head. "No, unfortunately, he didn't. After his freshman year, he came home for the summer. He'd been offered a summer job doing research for one of his history professors, but he turned it down because his father said he could use his help in his repair shop. I think his father wanted to remind Lou where his roots lay. Lou promised his father he'd come home and work with him during the three-month break. It would never have occurred to him to say no. Even though Lou knew his father was incapable of understanding him and his dreams for a better life, he felt indebted to him. So he came back to New Bedford when the semester was over, set to work in his father's shop, and started hanging out again with his old high school buddies. Pretty soon it was as if he had never left, and he found himself staying up late at parties on the weekends and occasionally drinking too much. Now this all would have been harmless enough except for something that happened on one of those weekends, at one of those parties, when he had had one too many beers. It happened because for about fifteen minutes he let his guard down."

Constance took another sip of her wine.

"The one thing Lou had learned growing up in New Bedford was that the fastest way to ensure that you never left town was to get a girl pregnant. In a flash, you had a wife, then a child, then a growing family to support, bills to pay, groceries to buy, and a mortgage to worry about. 'I was not,' I remember Lou telling me, 'I was not going to ruin my life because of sex. But then I did.' He'd been very careful with girls throughout high school, never promising them more than he could deliver, never pushing, never expecting anything in return. He wasn't a priest, but he was a good boy. Careful. Cautious. Then one night he was at his best friend's house, a guy named Ted Jenkins, or Jenks for short. He was sitting in one of the new La-Z-Boy recliners Jenks's father had just bought and relaxing after a long week of working side by side with his workhorse of a father. Mr. and Mrs. Jenkins were out of town that weekend visiting Mrs. Jenkins's sister in Florida, and there was a lot of, as they used to call it in those days, petting and necking going on."

Constance shivered. "It's such a bizarre word, *petting*. But that's what they called it. That was the slang in those days. Anyway, Lou was not looking to score that night, as we might say today. Several of his friends had already had to get married, and, as I said, he was determined not to follow in their footsteps. He was always very careful, especially since the opportunities were always there, everywhere, all around him. He was actually half asleep when he noticed a girl in a yellow sundress standing over him. He lifted an eyelid and then another eyelid, and slowly, like the image in a telescope trained on a distant star, a girl named Irene Cavendash came into focus. Irene was a girl in the class ahead of Lou. They had dated casually a few times in high school. She was smiling at him in a steady, unblinking, inviting manner that set the hair on the back of his neck on end."

"Irene?" he said. "What's wrong?"

"What do you mean, what's wrong?" she asked.

"Why are you looking at me like that?"

"Like what?" she said innocently.

"Like that?" he said, pointing a finger at her.

"I'm not looking at you any way," she demurred.

"Lou laughed, and Irene balanced herself on the arm of the La-Z-Boy and continued to examine Lou as if she were trying to memorize his face. Then, when someone brushed past her, she fell into his lap. The lights had been turned low to facilitate the furtive petting taking place in the dark corners of the room, and before Lou knew it, he was kissing Irene as if she were the last girl in the world. Then, as if in a dream, Lou told me, Irene led him out of the house and into the backyard. And there, under a thick covering of lilac bushes, she stripped off her dress and undid her bra. 'Let's play *almost*,' she whispered into his ear, pulling him down on top of her. It was only the second time Lou had ever seen female breasts, so before she could get her underpants off, the game was over. The moment of truth had passed. The next morning, when Lou woke up, sprawled across the sofa bed in his parents' living room, he could hardly remember what had happened. He remembered Irene Cavendash and her yellow sundress, some grappling in the woods, and a feeling that something had both happened and not happened. But it was all unfocused and unnervingly hard to remember.

"He didn't hear from Irene for a month after that night. He didn't see her around town or at any of the weekend parties. Then one afternoon she showed up at the repair shop and said she needed Lou to drive her to the doctor's office. 'Okay,' Lou said. 'If you need a ride.' He asked his father for an hour off and his father, eyeing Irene apprehensively, nodded for him to go on. As they drove to the doctor's, Lou threw a few sidelong glances at Irene, who was sitting, a model of perfect calm, in his broken-down Chevy, staring at the road in front of her. He wondered what was wrong with her.

"After the appointment, she came sailing down the sidewalk. 'Congratulations! You're going to be a daddy,' she told him."

"But we didn't even . . ." he said.

"But we did," she corrected him. "We did. You are going to be a father."

"But I . . ."

"We're going to be parents, Lou. We're going to get married."

"The next month was, Lou told me, a waking nightmare. When he finally brought himself to tell his parents, they were shocked. 'What about all your big plans for the future?' his father demanded. 'Yes, what about your dreams?' his mother echoed, and began to cry. When he went to Irene's father and asked for her hand in marriage, Mr. Cavendash was unmerciful. 'I just hope,' he snapped, 'that you don't mess up the rest of your life the way you've messed this up.' When Lou delivered his vows, his left leg was shaking uncontrollably, he told me, because he knew he was making the biggest mistake of his life. 'The minister had to repeat everything twice because I couldn't get the words out of my mouth,' he said. When they were pronounced man and wife and the minister told him, 'You may kiss the bride,' he stared blankly at Irene for a few seconds and then led her out of the chapel like a Boy Scout helping an old lady across the street. Everyone was hissing at him to kiss her, but he didn't hear a word. He was in a complete fog."

"But, Constance, why did he marry her," I asked, "if he knew it was such a big mistake?"

"Because it was the right thing to do," she said matter-of-factly. "Lou told me Irene was a 'nice girl,' and he couldn't abandon her. It was the ethos of the time—you got a girl pregnant and you married her. No questions asked."

She paused for a moment and seemed to be turning a number of things over in her mind. "But that wasn't the only reason. He could certainly have questioned the paternity of the child, but he didn't. And he didn't because he was following a pattern. I'm sure of this. He was doing the same thing his father had done twenty years before when he'd married his mother, who had also been pregnant. She'd been pregnant with Lou. And in that case, too, the question of paternity was never fully satisfied."

"Really?" I said.

Constance nodded. "His father had been traveling; there was another man. His mother may have been trying to make him jealous, and then things got out of hand. What's so interesting, though, is that Lou never knew anything about this until after both his parents were dead. He was going through his mother's things and found an old diary in the bottom of a box of photographs in her closet. There was a letter tucked in the back of the diary that his mother had written to this man explaining that she was pregnant. A letter it seems she never sent."

"So Lou got himself into the same situation his father did . . ."

"Without knowing about his father's situation. Yes, I mean he didn't *know,* but he knew. You can never keep a secret from a child. If they don't realize the secret consciously, they'll simply live out the secret unconsciously. It will become their life. And Lou's father's secret most definitely became Lou's life.

"Soon after Lou's first daughter, Angela, was born, a second daughter, and then a third, came along within the first five years of their marriage. Lou was on his way to re-creating the family he had grown up in when he had his first revelation, his first glimmer of understanding. He began to see what he was doing. He saw the pattern, or at least a big part of it. After that, he said to Irene no more children.

"You have to give him credit for this. Family patterns are very hard to break, almost impossible. There is an implacable desire in the human heart to repeat the past at all costs. We all do it in an effort to understand the second time around what we failed to understand as a child. Lou's only problem was that he didn't see this earlier, before the damage had been done. He was miserable with Irene right from the beginning. He felt trapped and suffocated. He couldn't even carry on a decent conversation with her. She belittled his interests. But the line had been crossed. He was married with a child, and then another child, and then another, and he had no choice but to make the best of it. And he did. He managed, by working all sorts of odd jobs and never sleeping, to graduate from Yale. He even went on to get his doctorate and to teach. He became one of Columbia's most prized professors, and now here he is, the CEO of the most in-fluential venture capital firm in the city, maybe in the entire country."

"And the envy of all his peers," I added.

She drew herself up in her seat.

"He's achieved a lot," I said.

"It's funny that you should say that."

"Well, he has."

"No, I mean about him being the envy of his peers." She folded her hands in her lap. "Lou always tells me that he envies me . . . that he envies me."

"Why?"

"Because I've had the freedom to make choices in my life. He feels as if all his choices were made for him. 'Every damn one of them.' At least, that's what he says."

I was about to disagree with her when, in an apparent at-tempt to head off my comments, she added: "I'm afraid he's a bit of a martyr sometimes. It's a problem. Now that his children are grown, he could change his life. There is nothing really stop-ping him, but he still thinks he's trapped. He still lets Irene call the shots. Since that first fateful night, he's put his life completely in her hands. She controls everything. She has him under a dark spell—a spell I have not found a way, despite his love for me, to break."

She studied me for a moment to see how I was taking all this in. Then, as if to soften the concerned look on my face, she said, "But I know it's not my problem to solve. It's his."

"That's right," I said. "You should try to remember that."

"But I have a great deal of faith in him," she said, brightening. "I know he can do it. I believe in him. I love him. I just have to be patient. It's funny, he's come to terms with his own internalized ideas of conventional morality, and he's gotten past the fear of appearances and what people might think about him being with a younger woman, but he still hasn't succeeded in getting past her. But he will. I'm sure of it." She tapped her clasped hands together on the edge of the table to punctuate this last statement. "Being conscious and self-aware is completely against nature, you know," she added, as if she had forgotten to impart this key piece of information. "You don't see the animals doing it. They just are what they are and do what they do. They don't think about it. Neither do most human beings. Neither did Lou."

"Until he met you."

"Until we began talking about it. I told him I thought he came home after that first spectacular year at Yale and got himself into trouble with Irene because, despite all his success at school, he was longing for the familiar, and for someone who would allow him to begin the long, absorbing process of recreating his past. It just so happened that that someone ended up being Irene. That was the attraction she held for him."

"And you told him all this?" I asked her. I wasn't sure how

you would go about telling someone that he's been living most of his life on automatic pilot.

"Of course I did. Why wouldn't I?"

"I don't know," I said, imagining that she must have seen it as her duty to be honest with him. "So what did he say?"

"He resisted the idea at first, but then he admitted that I was right. 'I thought,' he said ruefully, 'that I was the master of my own house.' He always has the ability to see things about himself when we're together, and I admire him for that. He's very open to looking at his own history."

"But he can't expect you to be there forever pointing things out to him."

"I know that," she said rather too forcefully, and then added, "I know. He has to see things for himself, and he will."

A shroud of deep confusion fell over her face then.

"You see, if we really want to live our own lives," she said a bit anxiously, "we have to break with the past once and for all. I did that a long time ago. When I was in college, long before I met Lou, I became infatuated with someone I met there who had an almost hypnotic effect on me. It was bewildering, and I never told anyone about it."

"Not even the guy?" I said.

"Definitely not," she said.

I wondered if she was talking about Nick Hutchins, Matt's friend. If I could, I would have asked her, but that would have been revealing a confidence.

"I realize now that I was afraid—of a lot of things—but mostly of making a mistake and ending up in an unhappy marriage like my parents. So, to avoid this, I pushed him away.

Of course, I didn't know it then, but that's what I was doing. I didn't want to repeat the past, so I behaved toward him as if I didn't care, and finally he went away. It was painful, but I decided, on some level, that I wanted something different, and I ended it. Lou, even at his age—and he's much older than I am—has yet to take that step. Irene is the demon goddess of his past, and the hold she has on him is deep-rooted and abiding. To break with her, he'll have to say no to her demands, to her guilt trips, to her unflagging attempts to convince him she's helpless without him. It's going to be very hard, but I know that one day soon he is going to be able to do it. I know. I told you, I believe in him. He's a strong man and very intelligent. He understands what he has to do to be free, to put the past behind him."

She absently fingered the stem of her wineglass, which was still full. "Of course, at this point, it isn't just Irene who is holding him back."

"What do you mean?"

"He has, as I said, three daughters, and now he has to also heed their siren call." She stopped herself. "I'm sorry. I'm being sarcastic, but it's hard sometimes. They're a handful. I used to have a great deal of sympathy for them, but now it's harder. The oldest, Angela, is completely dependent on him, both emotionally and financially. She's a single mother of four. The second child, Marianne, lives in San Diego and works at the San Diego Zoo. She is estranged from Irene and calls Lou at his office maybe once every six months. She loves animals. Hates people. The third daughter, Sarah, is an alcoholic and has spent her entire life in and out of rehab. It's as if each of his children were poisoned in some way by the silent animosity and gamesmanship that was always going on between their parents. And now Angela, his oldest daughter, has grown up to be a complete replica of her mother, where at one time, when she was younger, she had been Lou's best friend. This pains him no end. She actually uses her children to keep him in line. She reminds him all the time that if he ever leaves her mother, she'll turn his grandchildren against him. She'll never let him see them again."

"Really," I said.

"Yes, and that's very hard on Lou. He loves his grandchildren. He's been like a father to them. Without him, they'd be in desperate straits. Their mother has never worked. I think the problem is that Lou has been everything to Angela. He's been for her a father, priest, confidant, and counselor, and she doesn't want to lose him. She doesn't care whether he's happy or not. She just wants him there, where she can keep an eye on him. Lou told me she fainted when Irene showed her the photograph in the *Daily News*."

"She fainted?"

"Yes, she had to be taken to the hospital. Lou was quite shaken up about it."

"Did he actually tell Irene and Angela that he's in love with you?" I asked, thinking it would take more than a grainy photograph to make someone faint.

She shook her head. "No, he insisted we were just friends. He said he wanted to protect me."

And himself, Constance. He also wanted to protect himself, I thought, but I didn't say it. Maybe I should have, but there was something about her love for him that silenced me. It would have been like telling an innocent young girl that death will one day come and whisk her away, and I just couldn't do it. Instead, I asked her where things stood now.

"In limbo," she said.

At this point, I was leaning forward in my chair like an overeager reporter, ready to barrage her with questions. "But I haven't finished the story," she said, as if it wasn't time yet for me to begin drawing conclusions. "I haven't even gotten to the most dramatic part."

I sat back then and nodded for her to continue.

"By the time Lou and I met again at the 92nd Street Y, he and Irene were closing in on their thirty-fifth wedding anniversary and had been sleeping in separate rooms for more than thirty years. They were like a corporation. They came together only to discuss the children, finances, and their social schedule, which, as his prominence grew, became more and more consuming. She became his secretary, sorting through and accepting or declining the many dinner and party invitations that were deposited in their mailbox each day. She thrived on their ever-increasing social status and loved being seen in public in her new dresses and furs. They grew further and further apart, which was very far indeed, because they had never been close to begin with.

"Now, no one except Lou and Irene and their children knew about their problems. Some of their friends thought they were a little mismatched, but they never suspected that they led essentially separate lives, that Irene sometimes threw things at him when she was angry, that she often disparaged his interests, and that their intimate life was nonexistent. They were both very good at keeping up appearances. They both had to be, be-

Catherine Cantrell

cause it takes two in a situation like that to make it work. If one of them betrays the secret, the game is over. Irene resented the money Lou gave away to charity, and they argued bitterly over every donation he made, but when it came time to present the check, she was right there next to him smiling for the cameras. Everyone who knows her thinks she is a saint, and this pleases her very much. But even a saint has to have an outlet for the dark side of her personality, and Irene found that outlet in the terror she would wreak at home.

"He explained it to me once this way: 'When you are in a really terrible relationship,' he said, 'you wake up to it every day—constant contests and arguments over the littlest things. It's extremely tiring, but the years slip by and you become accustomed to it.' By the time he met me, he was quite inured to the daily battles and maneuverings that comprised their life together. He had learned to live with it by masking all his feelings and presenting a stoic, unflappable front to the world— something that has obviously served him quite well in business negotiations but has been anathema to his personal development. He sensed he was missing something, of course, and felt as if he were observing life through a thick glass wall, but it was a diffuse longing built out of unrealized dreams and vague imaginings. He'd had nothing to pin it to, nothing to embody his nascent emotions. He told me when he saw me sitting in the audience that evening at the Y, 'It was as if some lost part of myself had emerged out of the crowd to reclaim me. It was like finding a diamond in a pile of ashes. I was blinded with love for you; then I got to know you, and now I can see.' Of course, I didn't know that meeting me again had that impact on him. I would never have dreamed of it."

Constance shook her head back and forth slowly. "He told me within a week or two of our first dinner together that the first time I had walked into his classroom five years before, his heart turned over. He'd literally felt it in his chest—the sensation of someone reaching in and flipping it over like a pancake."

"I never knew that," I said to him.

"Of course you didn't," he told me. "You were a student."

"I know," I said, "but . . ."

"And now you're a woman."

She shook her head again. "He could say the most disarming things sometimes."

I smiled at the wonder in her voice.

"I think, now, that he told me all these things about his life because he wanted me to figure something out for him that he should have been able to figure out for himself but couldn't. I think he fell in love with me partly because he knew he could trust me to do this, and partly because I was observant enough to put certain things together."

"What do you mean?" I asked.

She looked up at me. "After we'd been seeing each other for about a year, and after he'd told me all of the things I just told you, I was in his office one afternoon waiting for him to get back from a meeting. On his credenza was a bunch of family photographs—group photos, photos of each of the girls, of Irene and himself, and of the grandchildren. I'd seen them many times before, but something made me start examining them. I looked at the photograph of Lou and Irene. It was probably ten years old. Then I picked up a photo of Angela when she was a teenager and another of Irene by herself. I started looking into their eyes to see if I could gain some insight into the personalities of these two women who had such a hold on his life. And then, like one of those hidden Magic Eye images, it popped out at me. Lou's and Irene's eyes were blue. Angela's were brown. Angela could not possibly be Lou's daughter. Everything I had learned about genetics in my high school biology class came flooding back to me."

Constance took a pen and a pad out of her purse and started sketching a diagram and talking about dominant and recessive genes and the various ways they could combine to produce eye color in a child. It was all a little confusing, but she clearly knew what she was talking about. "Facts are facts," she said when she was finished. "You can't argue with genetics. Angela's eyes are a deep, almost chocolate brown. Both of her parents' eyes are blue. Angela is not Lou's biological daughter."

She put her pen down.

"Of course, the ramifications of what I had discovered overwhelmed me. I began pacing back and forth in Lou's office, wishing he would return and at the same time wishing he wouldn't. I knew that the minute he looked at me he would know something was up, and I struggled to decide how I should respond. About ten minutes later, he came sailing through the door, and we had another conversation I'll never forget."

·   ·   ·

"Hello, sweetheart," he said; and then, the moment our eyes met, "What is it?"

I smiled tentatively and turned away from him toward the photographs. "I was just looking at these," I said.

He came over and took me in his arms. "Oh, those photos," he said. "They're mostly for show."

"They tell an interesting story," I said.

He held my face in his hands and kissed me. Then he gave me a long look. "You're a miracle. Do you know that? A god-damn miracle."

I smiled. "I'm a miracle, but, Lou, have you ever really looked at these photographs?"

He took his hands away from my face. "What do you mean?"

I picked up the photo of Angela. "Look at this picture," I said.

He put on his reading glasses and smiled. "She was pretty then, wasn't she?"

"Yes, she was," I said. "She has beautiful brown eyes, doesn't she?"

The smile on his face fell away and a studied tension formed around his eyes. "Yes, she does."

I picked up the photo of Irene and him. "I never noticed that both of you have blue eyes. Did you ever think about that?"

He scrutinized the photo.

"No," he said.

"Lou, it isn't possible. It isn't genetically possible for two blue-eyed parents to have a brown-eyed child. How did the two of you do it?"

His eyes grew wide and then seemed to collapse into his face. He put down both photos and went and sat on the couch. I sat down beside him. He seemed to have stopped breathing. I took hold of his hand, and he drew in his breath sharply and then expelled the air in his lungs slowly as if a thousand doubts and uncertainties were being released into the open air.

He looked at me. "Are you sure about this?"

"Yes, I'm positive. It's basic genetics," I said. "You always had doubts, didn't you?" I'd asked him this question many times before, but he'd always denied it.

He nodded his head slowly. "I had doubts, but I should have seen—"

"I think you just didn't want to see it," I told him. "It's very easy to overlook things when you don't want to see them. And it's always the things closest to us that are the hardest to see. They are so familiar they're virtually invisible."

He held my hand tightly, and we sat there for a long while adjusting to this new order of things.

"But Angela . . ." he said.

"Are you going to tell her?"

He shook his head. "No, if she figures it out one day for herself, fine, but I'm not going to be the one to shatter her world."

"And what about Irene?"

"I'm going to talk to her," he said firmly.

And he did. He got home late that night, he told me, and came in the back door and found her sitting in her usual spot at the kitchen table going through the mail. She was completely absorbed in what she was doing and didn't even notice he was in the room until he pulled out the chair next to her.

"The Wellingtons are giving a party next month for Senator . . ." she said, beginning her long litany of party invitations. Lou listened, feeling, he told me, as if he were leaning over the edge of an abyss. Finally, when she was finished, he spoke up. "Irene," he said, "I have something I want to talk to you about."

The tone of his voice must have told her that what was coming was not pleasant because she stood up and placed herself on the other side of the kitchen table, as if she found it necessary to put some physical distance between them.

"What is it?" she asked.

"I've been thinking about Angela's conception," he said.

She stared at him. Then she pulled out a chair and sat down again. "I was wondering when you were going to ask me about that," she said matter-of-factly.

.   .   .

Constance put the palm of her hand to her forehead in disbelief. "Can you imagine saying to your husband after thirty-five years of marriage, 'I was wondering when you were going to ask me about that'? I mean, it's so *dramatic*. It's like something out of a movie. 'I was wondering when you were going to ask me about that.' "

"Yes, I see what you mean," I said. "And then what happened?"

"Lou walked into the living room and brought back two photos, one of Irene and him and one of Angela, and laid them on the table in front of her. Then he explained what he'd discovered."

"What did she say?"

"At first, nothing. Then she picked up the photo of the two of them and slammed it down on the table. The glass broke apart like a sheet of ice."

"It must be true then," Lou said calmly.

"No," she said. "I'm just outraged that you would even think of such a thing."

"It's hard not to," he maintained, *"when the facts are staring you in the face."*

"I don't believe in your facts," she said.

"You don't believe in genetics?" he asked.

She turned to him. *"It just can't be,"* she said firmly. *"There wasn't anyone else."*

"There had to be," he told her.

She smiled sweetly. *"There wasn't."* Then she got up and poured herself a glass of water. *"I'm going to bed,"* she said. *"Good night."*

.   .   .

"And Lou let her go?" I asked Constance.

She shrugged. "Yes, he let her go. She went up to her bedroom and closed the door. Lou stayed downstairs, threw the broken glass in the garbage, and went to bed. But he didn't sleep much. He spent most of the night pacing back and forth and staring out the window. When he went down to breakfast the next morning, it was as if the conversation with Irene had never happened."

"And he didn't bring it up again?"

She shook her head. "No, he never brought it up again. He couldn't bring himself to push her further, he said. 'To have said any more would have been indecent,' he told me."

Constance brought the tips of her fingers to her lips and studied the air for a moment. "I sometimes think that he's afraid of her," she said, sounding for a moment more like a detective than a woman in love. "Irene is a lot smarter than Lou thinks. He constantly underestimates her. She knows how to push his buttons and how to make him feel guilty. She knows what to say to make him question himself. When it's convenient, she pretends to be helpless, she becomes hysterical, she throws things, but she's not really helpless. Lou says her greatest fear in life is not having an escort. That's where he comes in. That's his greatest role, he says. She throws dust in his eyes by first frightening him with her anger and then seducing him with her gentle diplomacy. She's brilliant, in her way. You have to give her some credit." Constance clasped her hands together. "And now we have the *Daily News* photo."

"And what was her reaction to that?"

"She's threatening war. She's ready to contact all the tabloids and tell her side of the story."

"But why?" I said. "If it's already in the tabloids?"

Constance shook her head. "I don't know. She's very angry. She wants to completely discredit him and all the good work he has done for people. She wants blood. I think that's why she got so furious when Lou asked her about Angela's paternity. That's her Achilles' heel, and she doesn't want it exposed. But Lou would never use it publicly against her because he loves Angela too much. He'd never hurt her in that way, and Irene knows it. She knows she's safe."

She looked at me.

"Irene knows how to manipulate him, and she is always one step ahead of him. She has, without him even knowing it, had her finger on his pulse for decades, controlling his every move. I think in many ways that *this* is the hardest thing of all for him to accept. Nobody likes to think they've been duped. It's much easier instead to pretend that things were better than they were, that they were really not so bad. Lou does this all the time. He'll start to wax nostalgic about things that never really happened, imagining that at one time, somehow, things were better. And then two weeks later, he's fuming about how terrible it was."

She smiled sadly then, and a hint of uncertainty came into her eyes as her attention drifted toward the pianist and his slow, almost mournful rendition of the old Jerome Kern standard "The Way You Look Tonight." She grew pensive, as if the song's simple, seductive lyrics were pulling her into a world she knew she needed to resist. A few moments later, she recovered herself and said she hoped Lou would work through these problems and free himself soon. "He often says he feels like an insect stuck in a web. His family and friends are this sticky substance he can't extricate himself from no matter how hard he tries. If he solves one problem, they simply spin another one. The alcoholic daughter has a breakdown, Angela loses another boyfriend, one of his siblings gets into financial trouble, the grandchildren start having trouble in school. Spinning, spinning, spinning. They're always spinning."

It occurred to me then that despite her probing intellect and considerable brainpower, she was dangerously, one might almost say fatally, idealistic. It seemed never to have entered her mind that most people would find it extremely difficult to live up to her formidable standards. Truth, I had to remind her, is not for everyone.

"I know," she said, as if she'd been told this before. "Lou says it's an acquired taste."

"I'd have to agree with him," I told her.

We both sat there for a moment pondering the exigencies of this hard fact of life.

"It sounds, Constance," I said then carefully, "as if he's living two lives. Are you sure . . ." I was beginning to feel afraid for her. She had elevated Lou to almost unearthly heights.

She put up her hand to stop me. "I know. Lou hasn't been able to bring these two sides of his character together yet. They're like oil and water. They just don't mix. He has to make a choice, and he hasn't been able to do this yet, but he will. I know he will. I've put my faith in him. I couldn't have fallen in love with someone who would betray me in the end. I know that." She smiled ruefully. "It's curious because he's so decisive in his professional life. Nobody is more so. He knows what he wants, how he wants it, and when. There's never any hesitation. In his personal life, though, he stands paralyzed between a sense of duty and an adherence to the truth in his own heart. Duty, of course, seems the safer route, but the truth can never really be avoided. He likes to think that it can be, but it can't. Like a weed, it will break through concrete if it has to. It will appear in unexpected places, in strange little accidents and mysterious illnesses, in mental lapses and untenable daydreams, in fear, guilt, anger, and depression. It can never be subdued. And a lie, no matter how fervently it is believed in, takes an inordinate amount of energy to maintain. It draws strength from every other aspect of your life and leaves you with a distorted view of the world. You find yourself living in a land where nothing really makes sense. And no matter how hard you try to make it make sense, if you don't see the essential truth, it never will."

She adjusted herself in her seat. "I remember getting a call from him once. He asked me to come down to his office *immediately*. I hurried down there, and when I walked in, he pulled me in front of the window and put his arms around me. 'I just wanted to watch the sun go down with you,' he said. I looked out the windows of his fifty-fifth-floor office, and we watched this big orange fiery ball disappear below the skyline." She paused for a moment as she took in the memory. "He made me feel the joy, the ecstasy of having a passion for someone. And he said many beautiful things to me, things that no man had ever said to me before." The magic he had invested in her life was almost palpable.

"Lou also helped me a great deal. I spent my adolescence and most of my twenties locked into a lot of negative patterns. It would take me too long to explain them all to you now, but sufficient to say, before I met Lou, I was always attracted to men who ignored me. Of course, I would never let them know that I was attracted to them, but I could never deny the fact that I was. They might notice me and even pursue me, but I knew, somehow I knew, that they never really wanted to know me. I was just an object. A pretty little statue they wanted to put in their trophy boxes. Lou used to spend a lot of time telling me how beautiful I was, but when he said it, it wasn't offensive. When he told me I was beautiful, he didn't just mean in the physical sense, he meant much, much more. My appearance mattered to him, but it wasn't the thing that mattered the most. He used to call it a nice bonus." She sighed. "Lou was my ticket out of a world I didn't want to live in anymore. He taught me that I could be valued for more than my appearance. So, in this sense I think of Lou as my savior, even though I know I'm really my own savior because I allowed myself to fall in love with him. I don't know who I would be if Lou hadn't come along. I feel that because of him I was able to break with my past. I'm free now, and I'm trying to return the favor by helping to free him."

"That's fine. But is that what Lou wants? Remember, Constance, you wanted to be free. You just said so yourself. That's why you fell in love with him."

"Yes, he does want to break out of the prison he's living in," she said. "That's why he was attracted to me in the first place. He's trying. But he's having a hard time. The spell he is under is very strong. He doesn't realize it yet, but it has nothing to do with fear of what other people will think, or the age difference between us, or his children, or questions of morality. It's deeper and more complicated than any of those things."

I gave her a puzzled look.

"When Lou met me he had really only known two women—his mother and his wife. His entire notion of relationships was predicated on his parents' marriage and his marriage to Irene. The concept of choosing to be with someone, not *having* to be with someone because of an accident or out of a sense of duty, was a novel idea to him. It still is. It is a mysterious, fascinating concept that has the power to utterly mesmerize him, when it isn't scaring him to death."

"And why does it scare him to death?"

"Because it's unfamiliar," she said, stating, in her mind, the obvious. "It's very hard to conceive of something that you've never experienced. As far back as Lou can remember, *no one* in his family has ever chosen to get married, including, as I said, his own parents. They've all had to get married for one reason or another, usually because of a pregnancy. It's sort of a legacy passed down from one generation to the next, like his blue eyes.

Choice. That's what he's wanted to have all his life. That's why he went away to college, to increase his options, but then he met Irene, and, well, I've just told you what happened."

"But he's a very successful man. He obviously made the best of it."

Her eyes brightened. "Oh, I know. He says, though, that he's achieved all he's achieved in spite of Irene, not because of her. She never made it easy."

"I see."

She took a deep breath. "I must say, it does feel good to talk about these things." She stretched her arms out in front of her like a dancer warming up before class. "I remember reading somewhere that a secret is by its nature isolating. Lou and I have had each other, but I've often felt isolated. I think he does, too, sometimes. It's difficult."

"Of course it is," I said.

"I just didn't want you to think that this was a simple case of older man leaves wife for younger woman. It isn't. I want you to understand that."

"I understand. Now, the question is, what do you do now? What do you want to do?"

"Nothing, really. Just wait. I want to see what Lou decides."

"But you could make a decision."

"I know, and my decision is to wait." She glanced up at the ceiling. "I'm going to wait."

The tone in her voice left no room for discussion. Despite what she had said at the beginning of the conversation about needing advice, I could tell now that what she had really wanted was someone to listen to her. She did not seem the least interested in my take on the relationship. She just wanted me to know about it. She wanted a witness.

"I guess we're friends now," she said, bringing the palms of her hands together. "There must be some ancient Chinese proverb that says once you've divulged hidden truths about yourself to another person, you're connected to that person for life."

"There must be," I said, "and if there isn't, there should be."

She looked down at her watch. "It's almost seven o'clock. I'm sorry to have kept you so long."

"No, you haven't. Don't even think that. This has been very enlightening." I had no desire to leave her.

"If you have a few more minutes, then, I'd like to show you something." She signaled to the waiter for the bill, and after paying for both of our drinks, slipped the strap of her black leather purse over her shoulder and stood up. "We have to walk through the lobby."

I followed her out of the cocktail lounge and around the corner, past display cases filled with Cartier watches and Oscar de la Renta dresses, through the elegantly appointed hotel lobby with its overstuffed armchairs and Statue of Liberty–crested Waldorf-Astoria clock from the 1893 Chicago World's Fair, to a little village of shops in the back of the hotel. She stopped in front of a glass case filled with old, carefully preserved books. Each volume was standing upright with a small placard next to it describing its condition, the year it was published, and the price. If the author had inscribed the book, it was open to the page bearing the inscription so you could read it. Bauman Rare Books was printed in gold lettering on the top of the display window, and a fashionable young woman with tortoiseshell glasses was talking on the phone in a corner office in the back of the store. Constance's attention was immediately drawn to a small white volume on the display case's top shelf—a copy of Emily Dickinson's first book of poems. "It was published four years after her death," she explained. "Of course, the poems initially presented to the public were heavily edited. Higginson and Mabel Loomis Todd excised a lot of the dashes she was so fond of and added conventional punctuation and regularized many of the rhymes. It took almost seventy years before they were published as she had written them."

"A lot of those adulterated versions of the poems are still floating around out there," I pointed out, "because there are no copyright restrictions on them anymore."

"I know. It's a disgrace," she said, as if there were something obscene about this. "Only five hundred copies were originally published, and they created an immediate sensation. Then there was a second volume, and then a third. They're all, of course, valuable collector's items today."

The volume we were staring at cost $8,500.

"Her poems were fresh and imaginative," Constance continued. "They were unlike anything anyone had ever read before. That's why I admire her the way I do. She didn't alter her work to meet the expectations of her times. She was completely herself."

She moved quietly to the other side of the display case, and her eyes came to rest this time on a first edition of Sylvia Plath's *Ariel*. "Sylvia Plath's poems were published as she wrote them, but not in the order she wanted them to be read," she said. "When she died, she wasn't divorced yet, so her husband gained control of her estate. He, for whatever reason, rearranged them.

She wanted 'Wintering' to be the last poem in the book, so the collection would close with the lines: *What will they taste of, the Christmas roses? / The bees are flying. They taste the spring.* As it is, the book ends with the poem 'Words.' The last line in that poem is . . ." She thought for a moment. "The last two lines are: *From the bottom of the pool, fixed stars / Govern a life.* It makes it seem as if her whole life were leading up to her suicide—as if it were inevitable—but I don't think it was."

"Look," I said, pointing to a book in the corner of the bottom shelf. "There's a copy of *The Great Gatsby*." The book was sans the famous dust jacket with its mournful, heavily made up eyes and garishly lit New York skyline. The green clothbound volume had a price tag of $1,400.

"When Fitzgerald died," Constance said solemnly, "there were still piles of unsold copies in the Scribner warehouse." She studied the book carefully. "I think he knew, though, what he had accomplished. He must have known."

The reverence in which she held these books made me feel as if we were in a church. She let out a deep sigh then as if she had finally found a space to release the tension and anxiety of the past few weeks. "Whenever I feel overwhelmed with my life," she confided, "I walk over here and look at the books. I find it very relaxing. When you think about all the problems and difficulties each one of these writers endured, my problems suddenly seem almost trivial. It all passes eventually anyway. The only thing that really matters is the work you leave behind." She stared at the books behind the glass as if she found incalculable comfort in their immutability and in their very bookness—in the paper and ink and thread and glue that held them together.

She turned to me then. "I had better let you go. Thank you

for listening to me, and please, Morgan, keep my confidence. I've put my . . ."

I reached out and touched her arm. "You can trust me, Constance."

"I know," she told me. "I'm not sure how everything . . . No, I know everything is going to work itself out, but this is a difficult time." She pulled a manila envelope out of her purse. "I have another story poem for you. Maybe when I get these out of my system, I'll be able to write my novel."

She handed me the envelope. I opened it and pulled out a long poem entitled "A Flock of White Doves."

"Thank you," I said. "I'll let you know what I think."

She nodded, and we walked back through the Waldorf's famed Art Deco lobby in silence. As we passed under the crystal chandelier at the entrance to the hotel and descended the broad staircase to the revolving doors below, she said, without looking at me, "Lou told me once that if you can go up and look at a problem from twenty thousand feet, any problem is solvable. I just don't seem to be able to get high enough to solve this one."

I gave her a sidelong glance. "Constance, why the sudden outpouring? You were so loath to say anything the last time we met."

"A reporter called my apartment last night," she said.

"What did he say?"

"He asked me if I wanted to verify some facts."

"What did you say?"

"I said, 'No, thank you,' and hung up."

I smiled. "You did the right thing. I'd advise you to lie low."

"I think Lou's wife tipped off the newspapers."

"She would intentionally put her dirty laundry right out there?"

"As long as she can position herself in a positive light," she said, "and you know that won't be hard. The wife is always the victim. The story never changes."

"I think it changes very slowly."

"Too slowly."

After we passed through the revolving doors, I asked her something that had been on my mind for weeks. "Constance, did you know that Lou is on the Peabody & Simms board?"

"Yes, he told me after I told him I had written to Matt. I thought it was an interesting coincidence, but then he's on a lot of boards. He told me the other day he's trying to cut back."

The ease with which she divulged this information led me to believe that she was telling the truth. She had, after all, no reason to lie. But it also made me wonder how many other things there were about Lou that she didn't know. Maybe there weren't any, and maybe there were many.

.   .   .

Before I went to sleep that night, I wrote down much of what we'd discussed because it seemed important, for some reason, that I remember it. Perhaps it had to do with the confidence she'd put in me. I was a custodian now, and I knew, somehow, that if I didn't commit this story to paper, it was going to fall, inevitably, into the cracks and recesses of my memory, and I'd never be able to find it again.

8

Within a week, Constance and Lou became a staple of gossip-mongers in New York City. Lou's celebrity was not of movie star caliber, but if not on that vaunted level, it was certainly on the level just below that and growing. His reticence, instead of protecting him from people, only served now to make him more mysterious and, therefore, more intriguing. The pedestal he had built for himself was so high that when he toppled, the thud could be heard for miles around. Journalists and photographers began hunting him down with the unrelenting determination of hired guns.

Every day brought "new" revelations. The newspapers specu-lated about Constance's history, her age, her profession, her motives, how she and Lou had met, and what the future might bring. Almost all of their speculations were wrong. She did not come from a wealthy family on the Upper East Side, she was not in her early twenties, she had never been employed by Morgan Stanley or Kidder, Peabody, she wasn't looking for money, and she and Lou had not met at a cocktail party for underprivileged children at the Plaza hotel. The only thing that conformed to known fact was the abstract nature of their future.

It wasn't long after our meeting at the Waldorf that I received another call from Constance. She told me she had an unusual favor to ask me.

"What is it?" I asked.

There was a long pause.

"Just ask me, Constance. The worst thing I can do is say no."

"And I want you to say no if you feel uncomfortable."

"I can't know if I'm going to feel uncomfortable until you ask me," I pointed out.

"I was wondering if you would go to dinner with us," she said, letting the request hang on the line for a few moments. "Wherever I go, there are photographers trailing me. Their persistence is amazing. I don't even like going out anymore, and I'm beginning to become a recluse. I thought maybe if you went with us, and we all met at a restaurant, it wouldn't be so noticeable."

"I wouldn't count on it," I said.

"But, Morgan," she pleaded, "he told me he would like to meet you. Please say you'll come."

Her plaintive tone of voice acted like an elixir promising eternal gratitude if I acquiesced.

"Where and when?" I said.

"At Ruth's Chris Steak House on West Fifty-first Street, between Sixth and Seventh. It's on the south side of the street."

"When? What time?"

"Tomorrow night at seven-thirty."

I wrote it down.

"And, Morgan," she said.

"What?"

"Please keep an open mind."

"My mind is always open," I reminded her.

"Yes, you're right," she said. "That's what is so interesting about you."

The next day, after work, I walked over to the aforementioned Ruth's Chris Steak House. It was appropriately discreet, heralded by nothing but a black awning with the name of the restaurant printed on it in red and white block letters. Its exterior melded into the apartment complex that weighed down overhead, but inside, the atmosphere was reminiscent of a turn-of-the-century gentleman's smoking room. Dark wood paneling, gold and brass fixtures, and dim lighting all conspired to instill a feeling of relaxation and safety. When I told the host and two reservationists leaning over the front desk that I was meeting Lou Ellis and his dinner guest, their eyes brightened, and I was escorted to a table in the back corner of the dining room. Lou and Constance were already there, immersed in conversation.

Lou stood up and offered me his hand. Constance remained seated. "I'm so glad you could come," she said.

"I've heard a great deal about you," Lou told me, his penetrating blue eyes and firm handshake radiating a sense of power and ease.

I smiled and said I hoped what he'd heard had been positive.

"It has been very positive," he assured me and then had the waiter take my drink order.

"We were just talking about the renovation of Grand Central," Constance chimed in. "One of my favorite buildings in the city. I was about to ask Lou how much he thinks it would cost to build Grand Central today." She turned to him again. "So, how much do you think it would cost?"

He sat back and his tan features tightened as he tried to come up with an estimate. "A billion, at least."

"It would cost two billion dollars to build it today. It cost eighty million back then."

"*Really*," he said. "When was it built?"

"It was completed in 1913. It took ten years to build. There was an article in *The New Yorker* about it. I don't think you could get financing today to build a structure like that, booming economy or no booming economy. It would be deemed impractical. I used to think that they were able to put so much into buildings then because things were cheaper, but eighty million dollars is a lot of money even by today's standards. I think it must have been important to people then to create beautiful buildings. It was just part of the culture—the Beaux Arts tradition. In those days, the turquoise ceiling and its celestial design were merely functional. It was supposed to be a temporary fix until a skylight could be put into place and an office tower built around it, but then they ended up leaving it."

"That's true," Lou said, "but there is more to it than that. Grand Central was originally the point of origin for transcontinental railway travel. It was a stomping ground for the rich and famous. The Vanderbilts had put a lot of money into the railroads, and they wanted to make sure they created something very grand and impressive to showcase their efforts. It wasn't *merely* a commuter railway station back then."

"Yes," she said, leaning forward. "The commuters in those early days were banished to the lower level. They could enter the station and exit the station without ever coming upstairs. Keep the masses out of sight! That was the motto then." Constance smiled slyly, with a glint of wicked delight in her eyes, and Lou looked fabulously amused.

"She keeps me honest," he said, as he reached out and put his large hand over her delicate, pale fingers. Constance looked up at him slowly, then drew her hand back into her lap as if she didn't want to embarrass me.

I found it curious that with all the gossip and rumors whirling around them they could be sitting here calmly discussing the renovation of Grand Central Terminal. It made no sense until I realized that a large measure of the pleasure they took in each other's company stemmed from conversations just like this one. The intellectual bond was as strong as the emotional, and these two sides of their relationship were inextricably linked. The one did not exist without the other.

"It's good to see you here tonight, Mr. Ellis," our waiter said, nodding politely. "Are you ready to order?"

We all looked up at him, and I told them to go ahead while I examined the menu. Constance gave the waiter her order as if she were reciting it for the hundredth time. "I'm a creature of habit," she said afterward. "I always get the same thing, unless I'm feeling particularly daring, in which case I get the broiled tomatoes instead of the asparagus."

"That is daring," I said.

"They're excellent. They slice a big beefsteak tomato in half, slather it with butter, and sprinkle brown sugar on top."

I ended up ordering exactly what she had ordered.

Lou looked very distinguished that evening in a dark charcoal-gray suit with a white shirt and a burgundy tie. There was something about him, with his naturally tan skin and good manners, that seemed faintly European. Constance was wearing a sleeveless black wool dress with a pink pashmina shawl draped over her arms. Her diamond pendant glowed in the lamplight. I could see the men at the other tables eyeing her appreciatively. She was completely oblivious to the attention. Her entire being was focused on only one man.

Looking at the two of them, I thought, "Here is a classic combination—beauty and power, in equal measure." But it didn't take me long to see that although they filled these stereotypical roles perfectly, they themselves were not stereotypes. Lou wore his power lightly, and Constance's beauty emanated from within. Her fine bone structure seemed almost incidental.

"So," Lou said, sitting back in his chair, "I understand that Constance and you have been working together."

"Morgan is giving me a lot of guidance," Constance said. "She's a gifted editor."

"So I've heard."

"I've talked about you *a lot*," she explained.

This surprised me. In my mind, the world I inhabited and the world Lou inhabited were so separate and far apart that it was hard to envision them intersecting at any point, even if that point of intersection was Constance. But then I reminded myself that she had that unusual ability to make the impossible seem fairly ordinary. So maybe it wasn't so strange, sitting across from Lou Ellis, one of the most influential businessmen in the city, and Constance, at the Ruth's Chris Steak House in the heart of midtown Manhattan, being told that they talked about me *a lot*.

"What do you think, Ms. Clifford, of Constance's writing?" Lou asked me.

"Please, Mr. Ellis, call me Morgan," I told him.

"And please, Ms. Clifford, call me Lou."

"I think she has a special voice, and I hope she'll put it to the test in a novel."

"I am trying," she said, "but my mind is set in its ways—very set in its ways."

"Maybe there is such a thing as trying too hard," I offered. "You have to let your unconscious take the lead." I was beginning to worry that part of her problem was that she was thinking about it too much. It is never productive for an artist to be self-conscious. Self-aware, yes, but never self-conscious.

"No," Constance said firmly. "My problem is that I'm too dependent on my unconscious. I have to learn to think through what I'm doing instead of just jumping in without any conception of where I'm headed. I'm never going to get anywhere if I keep doing that."

"Yes," I conceded, taken aback a bit by her vigorous response. "You do need to have a certain structure in mind when you write a novel."

"Of course you do," she reiterated. "I had an English teacher in high school who used to say, 'In every great work of art, there is a discernible structure.' We spent an entire semester meticulously analyzing *Wuthering Heights, Don Quixote,* and *A Portrait of the Artist as a Young Man* solely in terms of their structure." Her eyes drew away from us then and drifted toward that invisible world that always seemed to be within her view. "It was one of the most exciting periods of my life. I'll never forget it. It's the structure of a work of art that reveals its meaning. It all comes down to finding the proverbial figure hidden in the marble. I think when I can do that, when I can really see what I'm trying to get at, I'll be able to move ahead, but I'm not there yet. It takes time." Her brow tightened then, and she looked at Lou as if he, better than anyone, understood what she was trying to say. "It's a mysterious process. I remember working long hours on my poetry with little to show for it, and then one day it finally started to flow, and I started writing, really writing. I think artistic creation obeys its own laws. You can never force it. You have to be patient with yourself sometimes."

"It will come," Lou said with complete confidence. His unbounded faith in her was moving.

She gave me a knowing look. "He thinks of me as an investment. He expects high returns."

"I know a good bet when I see one," he said.

"Yes, I'm a one-person start-up." She eyed him steadily. "I'm just hoping I won't be sold off."

He shook his head. "Never."

"I think," I said, turning to Lou, "you've made a good investment. I think she's going to do it for you."

"She'll do it for herself," he said. Their eyes met again and a current opened up between them that, like a sudden flash of lightning in a dark, moonless sky, lit up the corner of the room where they were sitting.

Our waiter returned with a large round tray of sizzling steaks, red juicy tomatoes, and green beans. "Please hold your napkins up, folks. These plates are very hot." We all followed suit and silently watched him lay the plates round the table.

"Would you like anything else to drink?" he asked us.

Lou looked at Constance and me. "I'll have a glass of Chardonnay," she said.

I ordered a kir.

"And I'll have a glass of Pinot Noir."

"Yes, sir."

"Thank you," Constance said.

We waited for our steaks to cool and divvied up the vegetables. "These exquisite tomatoes remind me of a still life I recently saw at the Met," Constance told us. "Did you know that in French the term for still life is *la nature morte?*"

"Hmmm, dead nature," said Lou.

"I don't think the French have as many words as we do," Constance continued. "I remember there's a scene in *Sophie's Choice* where Sophie talks about the number of words in the English language for the word *vélocité*. She says there are too many to choose from. I think I'm fortunate that my native language is English. It's such a beautiful language to work in. Of course, French is beautiful, too."

"The French are very protective of their language," Lou added, as he cut into his tomato. "There are laws in France that limit the amount of English-speaking programming on the radio and television and that require advertisement and product labels to be in French. They've also made a concerted effort to create their own Internet jargon. Many people there feel that if they don't create a French-language presence on the Web, it could be a blow to the future of their native tongue. All the young people will be forced to use English."

"French, though, is the language of the stars," Constance declared dreamily. "There is a whisper of eternity in its rhythms that is reason enough for preservation."

"You should be working for the French ministry of culture," Lou said, before tasting his tomato.

"I was reading one of Baudelaire's poems the other day in *Les Fleurs du Mal* called 'The Love of Deceit,' 'L'Amour du Mensonge.' There's this strange image in it of a narcotic rose: *Oreiller caressant, ou corbeille de fleurs?* Caressing pillow, or narcotic rose? It's an interesting translation of that line. I kept lingering over it. There's something very disturbing about the idea of a narcotic rose. A rose is so beautiful, but I guess beauty in a weak mind can act like a drug. The poem is about a prostitute, I think. It's a very objectified portrait, but, of course, it's generally known that Baudelaire had some issues as far as women were concerned." She emphasized the word *issues,* giving me a conspiratorial smile, as if she knew I would fully understand her meaning.

Her comments on Baudelaire started me thinking about those four lines at the end of her poem "Long Before Christmas Morning"—the ones that had captured my attention on my trip to Boston. I could still remember them:

> These are the questions I have to ask.
> God is sometimes very hard to hear.
>
> Somewhere a woman is posing for a painting.
> It helps to have you near.

I told Constance I had been intrigued by these lines, then I asked her a question that I very rarely, if ever, asked any of my writers. I asked her what the poem meant. Most poets would find a question like this abhorrent, but Constance was quick, even eager, to respond.

"I've spent a lot of time thinking about those lines," she

said, setting down her fork. "When I wrote that poem, I didn't understand them either. But after I took some time to think it through, their meaning finally became clear to me."

Lou and I looked at her. It was strange the way she talked sometimes about her work as if someone else had written it.

"*God is sometimes very hard to hear. Somewhere a woman is posing for a painting.* What is God?" She looked to us for an answer. "That's the first question you have to ask. God is, when you get right down to it . . ." Again, she looked at us.

"A higher power," I suggested.

"And what is power?" She turned to Lou. "What makes a lightbulb glow?"

"Energy," he said.

"Right. Energy . . . something we feel . . . that which animates our lives and makes us human. Without energy we can't blossom. We're like a seed thrown on a cement sidewalk. We're dormant, asleep, inactive. But what is energy really? Is it that different from what people call God? I don't think so. I have never, except maybe when I was a child, thought of God as an omniscient being sitting up in Heaven watching over everyone. That image, for me, is too concrete. No, I think God is an energy field that flows in and through and around all living things. But just as the energy in a piece of coal or wood needs a spark to release it, the energy in our own lives can become trapped in misunderstandings and outmoded values, in ways of looking at ourselves and the world that don't really mesh with reality and are, therefore, useless. And when this happens, we feel the absence of—and I use the term symbolically—God; we feel dead inside. If a whole society becomes trapped in this way, people start talking about the decline of civilization. Boredom sets in then, and people start to drift. They feel tired, depressed, anxiety-ridden. Nothing works anymore because they've run out of energy. That's what Nietzsche was talking about over a hundred years ago when he wrote 'God is dead.' He wasn't being literal."

She paused for a moment and took a sip of water.

"But where has God gone? Where is the energy we're so desperately seeking? The law of the conservation of energy says that energy cannot be created or destroyed but only transformed, so what happened to it? It didn't just disappear. I think the energy has simply changed forms. I think it is hiding somewhere, and our feebly educated minds are simply incapable of seeing where it is. As Emily Dickinson said, *Not "Revelation"— 'tis—that waits, / But our unfurnished eyes.* It might be inscribed in assumptions we've never questioned or viewpoints we've never been able to see beyond. It might be hiding in the images we have created but don't see into adequately. It might be hiding in the painting of a woman." She said this last line with a marked lift of her chin, as if she had just proven a vexing mathematical theorem.

Lou and I stared at each other with puzzled eyes. She was so sure of herself and what she knew that it was daunting to less self-possessed mortals. It was as if, for the last few moments, Constance had taken flight and soared far above us to a place we could only gaze at in wonder from the ground. She seemed to have a special capacity to see with her bird's-eye view far into the future. So far that what she saw there was completely beyond view.

She picked up her fork and knife then and began to cut into

her tomato, oblivious to the feeling of admiration and curiosity
she generated in her listeners. Within moments, she was on to
another subject.

"I took Lou to the Met to see *Madame X* a couple of months
ago. Have you seen that painting, Morgan, by John Singer Sargent?"

I tried to place it, shifting my thoughts accordingly. "It's the
redhead, isn't it?"

"Yes, the redhead in the black dress with the plunging neck-
line."

"I haven't seen it for a while," I said. "I think I studied it in
my art history class in college. It created some sort of scandal,
didn't it?"

"It was the talk of the Paris Salon of 1884," she replied. "It
created *quite* a scandal in its day."

Constance's eyes met Lou's, and artful smiles full of bottled-
up emotions and veiled feelings appeared on their faces.

"Madame Gautreau, the notorious Madame X," Lou added,
still staring at Constance, "had very pale skin with a faint lavender cast to it that she accentuated with white cosmetic powder."

"She was a rather exotic beauty, a parvenue," Constance explained, "whose excessively made up appearance aroused considerable gossip. Sargent became fascinated with her and asked
if he could paint her portrait. Of course, she said yes."

They were gazing at each other now as if they were reliving
in their imaginations some secret moment that no one else in
the world knew about or would ever know about. "He did numerous studies—more than for any other painting. It took a lot
of time," she continued. "The finished work was quite unlike

the languorous, indolent poses in the sketches Lou and I looked at afterward in the bookstore. Remember, Lou?"

He nodded that he did.

"The dress she is wearing in the portrait has two thin diamond straps that hold up the bodice," Constance told me, but she was still looking at Lou. I wasn't sure at this point that she was completely cognizant of what she was saying. The words were moving through her now like a Shakespearean monologue through an actor. There was no hesitation, no subtle groping for the right words. It came out all of a piece. "In the original painting the strap on her right was falling off her shoulder. People, including Madame Gautreau and her mother, considered the portrait, and this one detail in particular, a terrible affront to decorum and vehemently protested its inclusion in the Salon. Sargent refused to withdraw the portrait, but afterward he grudgingly painted the strap back into its proper position. A photograph of the original painting survives, and you can see what it was supposed to look like. In the final work the right strap looks as if it were painted in hastily, perhaps in anger. There isn't the same attention to detail as there is in the left strap. Because of all the criticism, Sargent kept the painting hidden away in his studio for more than twenty years, but he considered it his masterpiece. He captured Madame Gautreau just as she was—lavender skin and all."

"That's a fascinating story," I said, as the painting began to materialize in my mind.

"Do you get to the Met often?" she asked me.

"Not as often as I'd like to, but now I want to go up there and look at that painting again."

"I love it there," she said. Then she reached out and touched Lou's arm.

"I told Lou I became a member of the Met. It's only eighty dollars a year for unlimited access to the museum. Lou told me that was fine. 'You can be a member, but you can't get any more involved than that,' he said, because 'the quickest way to sour a love affair with an institution is to become involved in the running of that institution.' What was it that you told me you got involved with, Lou, and it ruined it for you?"

Lou took a sip of his Pinot Noir and then set his glass down slowly. "The Boy Scouts." Constance and I looked at each other and burst out laughing.

"You see what I mean. And no institution is immune. Charities and philanthropies are sometimes the worst offenders."

He nodded in assent.

"If anyone knows that, it's Lou," she confirmed.

Finally, I saw an opportunity to make a contribution to the conversation.

"Lou," I said, "I understand that you have done a great deal of work for the disabled."

"Yes, I have," he said.

"Didn't you found a charity called Five Points? I believe I read about it in the *Times*."

He nodded. "It's not a charity so much as an assisted living program. We find jobs for handicapped individuals so they can feel like contributing members of society. We also provide support for the families. Being a parent to a disabled child can be very hard. It requires a great deal of patience."

"I can imagine."

"Sometimes the kids are abandoned," Constance added.

"Oftentimes, it's the fathers who can't handle it, and they disappear," Lou explained. "Other times, the child reaches adulthood and the parents simply leave town. Last week we found a thirty-five-year-old woman with Down's syndrome who'd been alone in her family's apartment for two weeks. Her parents had moved to Florida."

"And this was a wealthy family," Constance pointed out.

"What was she like when you found her?" I asked.

"She was scared," answered Lou. "Very scared. Distraught."

We talked for quite some time then about the high divorce rate among parents who have children with disabilities and the strain it puts on a family. I noticed that Lou did not use any euphemisms such as "special needs." He was very straightforward about everything and didn't have an ounce of sentiment in him when it came to the trials and tribulations involved. He said he'd had people come to him under the direst circumstances for advice about what to do with a severely brain-damaged infant who was on the brink of death. His counsel is always the same—let the child go, let nature take its course. He said people rarely take his advice, though, and they usually come to regret it. "It doesn't mean that they don't love the child," he said. "But the suffering is so great for everyone involved, especially the child."

On that solemn note, we completed our dinner, and our plates were cleared away.

"May I get anyone dessert?" our waiter asked as he handed around menus.

As Constance was praising the crème brûlée and the mixed berries with cream, the host came over, leaned down, and whispered to Lou that he had a telephone call. Lou looked mildly annoyed, but he politely excused himself and left the table.

"He's too much of a gentleman to have a cell phone," she explained. "Sometimes he has to leave a number where he can be reached. He's in the middle of closing a deal with a company that produces routers."

She said the word *routers* as if she knew exactly what a router did. I imagined she knew all about the World Wide Web and Internet start-ups and venture capital funding after being with Lou for two years. But I wondered how much Lou knew about her areas of expertise.

"Was Lou interested in literature and poetry before he met you?" I asked. "Or did you introduce him to all these things?"

She smiled and the warmth of her memories kindled the blue light in her eyes.

"Lou had poetic inclinations long before he met me," she explained. "I remember talking to him in his office one morning. He was sitting behind this immense desk, and I was sitting across from him asking him questions about the cultural implications of the Internet, when he suddenly opened a drawer and pulled out a file folder. He handed it to me and said, 'I've never shown these to anyone before.' I opened up the folder and found seven poems all carefully typed out on onionskin paper—his name printed neatly under each one. I sat there and read through them. The overriding theme was one of longing—longing for an intimacy that he had never experienced. One was called 'The Hour Before Dawn' and another 'The Memory of Rain.' They weren't great poems, but they were moving, and I could tell he'd worked very hard to find just the right images for the feelings he wanted to express. Naturally, I wondered who the poems were about.

" 'They're about you,' he said.

" 'But these were written twenty years ago,' I protested. 'The dates on the poems say 1977.'

" 'I didn't know you then,' he explained, 'but I knew I would someday.'

"So when we met again, it was as if he had been expecting me. I became the woman he had been waiting for, the woman in his poems. He showed them to me because he felt he had written them for me."

"Are you sure, Constance, that there have never been any other women?"

She nodded. "I'm sure. I know him too well now to even entertain that thought. Yes, I'm very sure. Believe me, I would know."

She seemed to understand my reservations, but I could tell she also wanted me to know that she could take care of herself, and that she wasn't one to be taken in by empty promises. I believed what she said about Lou, but more because of his spotless record than her assurances. If there had been someone else, I thought some plucky reporter would have dug it up by now.

"I asked him once," she said then, looking into her cup of chamomile tea, "what it felt like to fall in love for the first time at his age. I wanted to know what his reaction had been.

" 'I knew I wasn't dead,' he said.

"And then I asked him if he'd ever felt like giving up hope and just accepting his life.

" 'No,' he said. 'I knew one day you'd come.'

"He was very adamant about this. He told me confidently, 'I knew there was a great love in my future.' But other times he could get very frustrated and say, 'Before I met you, at least I had some peace in my life.' And the age difference bothers him now and then. He says it's not fair to me, but I tell him that's my decision to make."

She sat silently for a moment. "He was watching television recently," she continued solemnly, "clicking through the channels when he came across Franco Zeffirelli's *Jane Eyre*. He'd seen film versions of the novel before on TV, but this time he stopped to watch.

" 'Until I met you,' he told me the next day, 'I would have skipped right past it. Couldn't relate to it at all. Never gave it any thought. But now that I've known you, I found myself relating to everything. Scene after scene, I kept thinking, that reminds me of Constance. That reminds me of our relationship.'

"There's a passage in *Jane Eyre*," Constance said, "that I looked up after he told me this, a passage I remembered reading in high school. It goes like this: *Mr. Rochester was about forty, and this governess not twenty; and you see, when gentlemen of his age fall in love . . . they are often like as if they were bewitched.* I read it to him over the phone.

" 'Yes, that's exactly how it is!' he said. 'I am bewitched by you. I'm putty in your hands.' I'm telling you this, Morgan, because he tells me I have this amazing power over him, but in my mind he has all the power. He's the one who has to effect a change in his life for us to be together, not me. From my point of view, he holds all the cards, but somehow he doesn't see it this way."

Before I had a chance to respond and tell her I thought she

was absolutely right in her judgment of the situation, Lou returned and took his seat again. He reached his hand out instinctively and gently touched her arm. I found myself deeply affected by the rapport between them and by their unshakably high spirits, especially in light of the gossip brewing just beyond the gates, and I thought of something I had read once about the impenetrable mystery of intimate relationships. I realized that it is impossible for anyone to truly know what is between two people except the two people involved. We try, of course. We write biographies and memoirs and magazine profiles, and maybe every once in a while we illuminate some small corner of this mystery, but we never see it whole, and the mystery that we have unveiled often tends to obscure much larger mysteries, which leaves us more unsure of what we were about than when we began.

I also found myself feeling decidedly uneasy, as if underneath the sparkle and sheen of their obvious love for each other lay a forbidding darkness. A darkness that, like the deepest regions of the ocean floor, is completely impervious to the sun's life-giving rays.

"Did you hammer out the kinks in the contract?" Constance asked Lou.

"Everything is taken care of," he said as he pulled in his chair.

Constance turned to me. "Lou is serving as acting CEO for Parizan—a software development company that specializes in graphic interfaces, which Bartley & Ellis acquired about . . . six months ago?" She looked to Lou for confirmation. He nodded. "Lou took the stock from fifteen to sixty-five. Now they're selling it to Sun, but they want Lou to stay on and run it for another six months while they look for a new CEO."

"Are you going to?" I asked.

He shook his head and drummed his fingers on the table. "I'm going to act as a consultant for a few months. I'm willing to help them make the adjustment, but they have to learn to manage it themselves."

"I guess these small start-ups change hands pretty quickly nowadays," I said.

"Sometimes, but you have to remember that nine out of ten start-ups fail, and of those that make it, few have life spans of more than five years. The odds are very long."

"That's true," Constance agreed, "but your odds are better than average. Lou is like an artist when it comes to buying and selling businesses. He sees things that other people don't."

"I see some things," he said modestly.

"He sees everything," she whispered confidentially.

I could tell that the high regard in which Lou was held among his peers meant something to Constance. She was very proud of him. I personally found the conversation a little beyond me. It felt strange to be talking about a business as if it were an object for sale in a department store. I couldn't help thinking of the employees who were at the mercy of people like Lou. I found his position both enviable and daunting.

"Lou has a crystal ball back in his office," she said drolly, "and he uses it to see what the future will bring. When he sleeps, the theater of his mind opens up limitless possibilities to him. He even knows a few magic spells."

"You really have a crystal ball back in your office?" I asked him, joining in the conceit.

"Yes," he said, leaning back in his chair. "It's a big round one. I keep it under my desk. I use it to chart humanity's progress."

"Oh, progress," Constance said dismissively. "I think the idea of progress is a fallacy."

"It depends on how you define progress," Lou said. "If you're talking about science and technology, then it's fairly easy to chart."

"Not necessarily," Constance countered. Then she looked at me with a playful twinkle in her eyes. "What about medicine?" she said, as if she knew exactly which switch to flip to get him started.

"Medicine is a perfect example. Each generation builds on the work of the previous generation."

"Maybe they do," she said. "But maybe they don't, always. I read an article once that said a great deal of the medicinal knowledge that the Indians had built up over thousands of years was lost in a few generations. There are probably hundreds of plants out there that have curative powers we don't know anything about, but the Indians knew. I think in a lot of cases people build up knowledge and then it's lost, and they have to start all over again. Look at what happened to the libraries of the ancient world. They were almost all destroyed, and hundreds of thousands of scrolls were burnt or disappeared."

Lou weighed all this for a moment and then offered a more optimistic perspective. "But now we have the means not only to record knowledge but to create powerful databases that can store vast amounts of information, which can then be utilized in ways never dreamed of before. In the next five years, they will have mapped the entire human genome. That would not have been possible without modern technology. It is going to completely revolutionize medicine. That's progress."

"I think human beings do progress, but it is a painfully slow process," Constance said. "It's two steps forward, one step back. Of course, people are not put in jail for heresy anymore, but now we've gone to the other extreme. We have the hubris to believe that we can, with our science and technology, explain the world, that there are logical explanations for every single thing that happens to us. But sometimes those logical explanations are so tortured as to be unbelievable. Letting in a little mystery can often go a long way toward making sense of the universe. A thousand years ago people seemed to understand this. It's only now that we've forgotten." She paused then and looked at Lou as if she were remembering something disturbing. "Sometimes, when I'm sitting on the subway or flipping through a magazine, this awful feeling will come over me. I'll see an ad for a new miracle drug for depression or a pair of Manolo Blahniks, however you pronounce it, those shoes, photographed as if they were great works of art, and I'll feel as if I'm living in the midst of another Dark Age, and I just haven't realized it yet. In the early medieval period people forgot about the arts and learning and literature, but this seems a small thing compared with what we've forgotten today."

"And what have we forgotten today?" I asked.

Constance looked at Lou again. Then she looked back at me.

"That we have a soul, of course."

There was something about the way she said this that saved her from sounding like Deepak Chopra or Marianne Williamson. And I think what it was, was a certain spiritual integrity that had been painstakingly built up over the years like a pyramid. Each new insight had been like a stone cut and hewed to fit into an intricate structure. There wasn't a shade of embarrassment in her voice. In her mind, she was simply stating the obvious.

"In the future," she said, "I think this will be generally understood. People will look back on our time the way we condescendingly look back on earlier times, and see all our failings and wonder how we could have believed in the things we believed in." Constance looked at us steadily, and then her eyes settled on the candle burning in the middle of the table. "It's haunting to wake up in the morning and look out at a world devoid of mystery and magic. It freezes the heart. But the irony is that the world itself has not really changed, only people's view of it has changed. The opportunity for wonder and enchantment is still there. It always has been, and it always will be. It's just a matter of being able to see it, and sometimes that, I will admit, can be very hard."

Constance put her napkin down on the table then and excused herself to go to the ladies' room. "I shall return momentarily," she announced, as if she were reciting a line from a favorite movie.

She left, and Lou and I stared at each other warily. I could tell by the slight lift in his brow that he wanted me to like him and was hoping I might say something to ease his doubts. This vulnerability in a man of such power softened me a bit. "I see that Constance and you are very much alike," I began.

He looked at me questioningly.

"You're both passionate about what you do."

He considered this for a moment and then said, "I think that's what drew us together. She has an extraordinary mind. She sees things other people don't."

"Just like you do," I said.

"But it's different."

"How is that?" I asked.

"It's more important. My skill allows me to make money. Her skill allows her to create art."

"But you create jobs. You give money to charity. There is a certain symmetry there," I pointed out.

"Perhaps," he said, but I could tell he had never tried to equate the two.

"It's the differences you love the most, isn't it?"

He nodded. "She filled a hole in my life. I'd always wanted to be more involved with the arts, to get away from the business side of things. She opened up that world to me."

"And I'm sure you opened up new worlds to her, too."

"She says I have. She's a quick study. Picks up things just like that." He snapped his fingers. "Very curious. Always interested."

"So, you finally met your match?"

"Yes."

"There's something very gratifying in that, isn't there?"

As I said this, the battle scene between King Arthur and Lancelot in the film *Excalibur* popped into my mind. I could see Lancelot, after a long and dispiriting search for a worthy adversary, finally being, to his infinite delight, bested by King Arthur. I'd rented the movie after Constance had mentioned it at our first lunch together at La Réserve. She had a way, when she talked about a book or a movie or a painting, of making you want to run out and find the book, or watch the movie, or see the painting. I was rereading Emily Dickinson's poems and had completely immersed myself in *The Great Gatsby*.

"There certainly is," he said with that confident modesty that was the most potent part of his mystique and went along with everything I had ever read or heard about him. "It's extremely gratifying. She was the first person I ever met who was willing to take me on, to challenge me. She's not afraid to point things out when I'm not looking at something clearly, and she knows how to push back when she needs to."

"That's what happens when you become famous, isn't it? People shy away from criticizing you and telling you how they really feel." I knew from reading a lot of biographies of famous men and women that success, like a booster rocket, creates distance—lots of distance.

"I wouldn't call myself famous, but yes, it can become very isolating when you reach a certain level of success in your chosen field," he admitted. "It's unfortunate."

I couldn't believe at first that he wouldn't call himself famous, but then I guessed that it depended on how you defined the term. If you equated being famous with being a celebrity, then he undoubtedly fell short of the mark. If you equated fame with stellar achievement in a chosen field of endeavor, then the term applied magnificently.

"Lou," I said. "I hate to break this to you, but you're more famous than you might think. Your name appears in the newspaper at least once a week. I should know. I'm an inveterate reader of the *Times*."

He sat back and waved this away as if by depreciating it he could make it disappear, but I knew such conjuring tricks never work.

"I think you're both visionaries, too," I said.

"That's very important in business," he told me. "Leaders should, ideally, be visionaries."

"They aren't always, though," I pointed out.

"That's true, but if they're not, they need to have the intelligence to surround themselves with talented people."

"To make up for what they lack?"

"Yes," he said.

I sat there staring at him for a moment, wondering how a man of such commercial acumen and business savvy, a man so skilled at getting exactly what he wanted out of people, could be so deficient in his ability to pierce the bubble of hypocrisy that had blown up around him. I had a strong hunch, from everything Constance had told me, that his understanding of his motives in almost anything he did was dangerously limited. I didn't doubt his love and affection for her—that was impossible to miss. Even a practiced cynic wouldn't have been able to see past it. But I knew from experience that love and affection are never enough if they're not coupled with a clear view of the other person and an ability to honestly access the reasons for the mutual attraction, especially if that attraction is overwhelming, as I had no doubt Lou and Constance's attraction was. Lou was a man whose emotional life had completely split off from his family. It functioned in the small, perfect world he and Constance had created for each other. A world that, no matter how idyllic and nurturing, was not real. But it was his ability to move in and out of this world that allowed him to survive. Without her, his newfound emotions would have had no place to go. They would have submerged him in a sea of urgent desires and inchoate longing, and flooded his life with a restlessness he would have found difficult to control, let alone understand.

But it was these very floodgates that needed to open if he was ever going to change. Constance's patience and understanding were only keeping the waters of transformation at bay. But she couldn't protect him forever. At some point, he was going to have to look at his past and the choices he had made and ask himself the only question that really matters in the end, "Why?" And until he was forced to ask that question, he would have no trouble dining with Constance in the evening and returning home the next day to the sterility and security of his life with Irene.

Constance's vision of Lou was so bright that it completely blinded her to this dangerous fact. She saw only goodness and love in his eyes, but I saw something far different. I saw the desperation of a man who, tied to a woman he didn't love for thirty-five years and married to his work, knows in some shadow area of his being that his time is running out and he has missed something. Not love and romance, because he had found that with Constance, but something bigger. Something that, if seen and understood, could draw back, once and for all, the heavy curtain that hung between himself and his own life.

"She's an innocent, you know. Despite her intelligence," I told him.

"Yes, I know." He smiled, and a melancholy spirit invaded his eyes. "When we met, she had no conception of my financial status. I finally understood this when she kept refusing to take taxis. 'Too expensive,' she'd say. I'd press twenty dollars into her hand, and she'd walk five blocks and take the bus." He sighed as if the naïve obstinacy of the gesture still had the power to startle him.

"Lou," I said then, ready to broach a topic that had been suspended like an ax over our heads the entire evening, "I don't want to be rude, but it seems to me the pivotal question has not been addressed all evening."

"I know," he said.

"Are you leaving your wife for her?"

Lou hesitated, and in that hesitation I knew he had no intention of doing this. I sensed, though, that his inability to act had nothing to do with a lack of devotion to Constance or any feeling of respect he had for his wife, but seemed to stem rather from an amorphous fear of change. A curious quality in a man who had based his entire professional career on the concept.

·   ·   ·

Constance called me the next day to ask what I thought of Lou and to read me a poem she had just completed that seemed to especially please her.

"Lou is charming," I said. "I could see the glint in both of your eyes, but he is married, Constance."

"I know that," she said. "I know what I'm doing. Now, the last thing I need for you to do is to worry about me."

"Okay," I said. "I won't." But I did.

She ignored the concern in my voice and proceeded to read her poem to me, which seemed momentarily to have superseded even her interest in Lou. I remember the last few lines:

> Be careful of all the things you surmise with your
>   love for me.
> How do I explain to you that I live alone,
> That I'm not that well acquainted with the moon?

"It's very good," I said.

"I wrote it last night," she told me. "I felt inspired."

"Well, it's very good." I was still thinking, though, about her blinding faith in a man I was sure she couldn't trust, a man who, in reality, had no idea what he was *doing.*

"Thank you for coming to dinner last night," she said then.

"Thank you for inviting me."

There was a perceptible pause.

"Have you ever read Yeats's 'The Municipal Gallery Revisited'?"

"I'm not sure," I said, drawing a complete blank.

"The poem is about friendship. The last two lines are: *Think where man's glory most begins and ends, / And say my glory was I had such friends.*"

Implicitly, of course, I knew what she was trying to say, and, inspired myself, I told her, "It's so easy to be your friend. Never doubt that." This seemed to mean a lot to her, and I was grateful for that later, because it was the last thing I ever said to her.

9

It was only a couple of days later that I was sitting with Linda in my office going over the day's schedule when an urgent call came through to me from Lou.

"Constance is in the hospital," he announced without greeting or explanation.

"What? Lou. Why? What happened to her?"

"We were in a taxi," he said.

"Yes."

"We were in a taxi," he repeated.

"You were in a taxi."

"Yes."

"And . . ."

"I was rushing her. I had a dinner to go to. We were supposed to go to the ballet, but this dinner came up."

"And she couldn't go with you?"

"No," he said. I imagined that she had never been able to go to any of his many business dinners.

"I was dropping her off at Lincoln Center. There was a lot of traffic. I was rushing her."

"You were rushing her. I know. Then what happened?"

"She opened the door. I didn't see the car. There was a collision. This is unbearable. Impossible."

"Where are you?"

"St. Luke's–Roosevelt . . . on Fifty-ninth Street."

"I'm coming," I said. I quickly gathered up my coat and purse and told Linda I might be gone for the rest of the day.

"Is everything okay, Morgan?" she asked worriedly.

"I don't know. Please tell anyone who calls that an emergency came up. I'll explain it to you later."

I ran down the hall and bumped into Matt on his way back from his weekly breakfast meeting with the chairman.

"Constance has been in an accident," I blurted out.

"What!" he said. "Is it serious?"

"I don't know."

"Morgan, stop!" he yelled, and then, "Call me!" as the door to the reception area closed behind me.

As I pushed the button and waited for the elevator to arrive, I felt a yawning gulf open in my chest. I held my breath and clasped and unclasped my hands. The light above one of the elevator doors lit up, and I went and stood in front of it. As the car descended to the lobby, I began subconsciously to appeal to some higher power. I wasn't a churchgoer; I belonged to no organized religion, but I was a believer. Not in Jesus, or the virgin birth, or any of the multifarious god-men that human beings have put up on pedestals to worship, but of something out there that partook of an exquisite mystery. I saw Constance by now as one of the finest examples of this mystery, and I implored God to see her through this.

Something out there must have had mercy on me that disconcerting morning because as I hurried to the curb with my
arm outstretched, a cab immediately pulled up, almost as if it
had been waiting for me. Fifteen minutes later, I was threading
my way through St. Luke's–Roosevelt Hospital on the West
Side. After speaking to a weary attendant sitting behind a big
plate-glass window in the emergency room, I learned that Constance, after getting out of surgery, had been moved up to the
intensive care unit on the eighth floor. As I navigated the hospital's long sterile hallways, I remembered an article I'd read
recently in the *Times* that said patients sometimes contract in-
fections simply by being in the hospital. I imagined Constance
lying in her room with deadly pathogens floating in the air
around her, and I wanted to take her somewhere far removed
from doctors and nurses and illness and death. She didn't belong
in this place.

As I walked through the waiting area outside the ICU, I
couldn't help but notice two or three photographers lurking
outside the heavy metal doors that separated the ICU from the
hallway. A kind-looking nurse at the front desk pointed me in
the direction of Constance's room. I crept up to the door and
saw Lou at her bedside holding her hand. His back was to me,
and I stood in the doorway completely unobserved and watched
them as through a one-way mirror.

He was holding her hand in his hand and touching the tips of
his fingers against the tips of her fingers. Then he interlaced
their fingers together and kissed the back of her hand. He
smoothed her hair and caressed her cheek. She looked as if she
were sleeping. Except for a lavender bruise blooming on her left

forearm, I wouldn't have known there was anything wrong with her.

Lou then laid his head softly on her chest as if he were going to go to sleep himself and put his arm over her waist. I heard him whisper, "I love you, my beautiful girl. I love you, Constance." He began weeping then as if she were already gone. He must have known she was slipping away from him because a piercing buzz began issuing forth from the machine above her bed, and a cadre of nurses and doctors rushed in and pushed him aside. He stepped away from her, and when he turned around, the look of despair on his face reminded me of a statue I had once seen at the Met. An emotion that had before been safely encased in marble was now pulsing through this man standing in front of me. I instinctively reached out and held his arm. "I'm so sorry," I said and, as if I had suddenly become a doctor or nurse myself, guided him out of the room.

I pulled a chair from the nurses' station and squeezed his arm. He sat down. As I was trying to think of something to say, my eye caught sight of a man in a black knit cap peering through one of the small windows in the metal doors. My blood froze as I remembered the photographers I'd seen on my way in, and I slowly knelt down beside Lou.

"Lou," I said, "were there any photographers at the scene of the accident?"

He looked at me. "I didn't see any."

"Are you sure?"

He shook his head. "I don't think I would have noticed if there had been. I was just trying to get her to the hospital. She seemed fine. Shaken, but fine . . . I thought she was going to be okay. Then her stomach started hurting. She just collapsed."

"What did the doctor say?"

"Severe liver damage. It's all internal trauma." His eyes were bloodshot and his face was wan and pasty from lack of sleep. He put his elbows on his knees and held his face in his hands. "Jesus Christ."

I put my arm around his shoulders. I didn't know what else to do.

When the doctor came out I introduced myself. He asked Lou if Constance's mother had arrived yet.

He shook his head and stood up.

"I'm sorry," he said almost matter-of-factly. "We did everything we could."

Lou's knees buckled, and both the doctor and I moved to steady him. "We'll need a next of kin to release the body to the morgue," he continued.

I knew that to this doctor, with his battered clipboard and white lab coat, this was a grim but all-too-routine part of his job, and I couldn't honestly blame him for his coldness. But I felt suddenly protective of Lou, and I fixed the doctor with a meaningful stare and entreated him, "Give us a minute."

"Of course," he said, and stepped back and walked away.

The tears came silently now. There was something so unreal about the whole situation that I found myself feeling very much the dispassionate observer—watching, registering, surveying, recording. The whole situation seemed no more tangible to me than a movie.

"I want to see her," Lou demanded then, and stood up and

strode past me. I followed behind as if I were attached to him by
an invisible thread. There was a nurse in the room fiddling with
the machines when we walked in. When she saw Lou, she
opened her mouth to say something, but then seemed to think
better of it and quietly moved past us.

Constance's eyes were closed, and Lou took her left hand
and rubbed it between his own large hands as if he were trying
to warm it. Then he took her other hand and did the same
thing. "Such beautiful hands," he said softly. "So beautiful. So
very beautiful." He touched her cheek slowly and tenderly, and
stared at her as if he were waiting for her to open her eyes. Finally, he leaned down and whispered something in her ear that
sounded like "Wait for me, sweet princess." Then he pulled the
sheet up around her shoulders as if he were tucking her in for
the night, and kissed her forehead. He stood up then and stared
at her lifeless body for a few more moments before leaning
down again and kissing her softly on the lips, as if he might still
be able to magically awaken her.

After the photographers had been dispersed by security
guards, Lou left, and I waited at the hospital for Constance's
mother, Mrs. Louise Chamberlain, to arrive. Lou had called her
and told her Constance had been in an accident. He identified
himself as a friend. He hadn't wanted to distress Mrs. Chamberlain further by divulging the nature of their relationship. He
told me Constance had told him that her mother was a very
proper midwestern lady, who had never remarried after her husband's death.

As I sat outside the ICU waiting for Mrs. Chamberlain,
memories of the night my husband died swept through me.

That same strange mix of guilt and disbelief, sorrow and anger that I had experienced then, I experienced now, making it difficult to stay focused. I started to ask myself if I could have done something, if I could have somehow stopped this from happening.

Finally, a thin, willowy woman with shoulder-length white hair came around the corner. She was at least three or four inches taller than Constance and had greenish-gray eyes, but the flawless bone structure and pensive demeanor were unmistakable. I knew instantly that this was Mrs. Chamberlain. The anxiety in her face was obvious, but her eyes still sparkled with hope. I could tell she desperately wanted someone to come up to her and say, "Everything is all right; your daughter is going to be fine."

I approached her.

"Mrs. Chamberlain?"

"Yes?"

"I'm Morgan Clifford."

"Oh, yes." She smiled hesitantly. "Constance has told me a lot about you. Can you tell me where she is?"

I had an impulse to call back the doctor, but instead I took a deep breath and said, "I'm sorry, Mrs. Chamberlain. Constance passed away about an hour ago."

A pained look crossed Mrs. Chamberlain's face as if someone had just laid a hot iron on her back, and then she froze. When she started to list to one side, I took her by the arm and guided her to one of the waiting-room chairs and sat down beside her.

"It's impossible," she said. "I have to see her. Where is she?"

"Of course," I told her. "Let me get the doctor."

I hurried through the metal doors and told the heavyset nurse at the front desk that I needed to speak to the attending physician immediately. "Her mother is outside," I explained. She eyed me sadly and said, "I'll find him, dear. It will just take a moment." I nodded and went back out to Mrs. Chamberlain, who was now staring blankly at the wall. She was so still that I thought for a moment she had stopped breathing. I sat down again. "He'll be here soon," I said.

A few minutes later, the impassive doctor appeared once more. "Mrs. Chamberlain?" he asked.

She nodded.

"I'm sorry. We did everything we could, but there were massive internal injuries. Please come with me. I'll take you to see her." I helped her up from her seat, and the doctor awkwardly took her by the elbow and guided her out of the room. I heard him informing her, as they passed through the heavy doors, that there would be paperwork to fill out and they would need instructions about what to do with the body. I don't think she heard this last part.

I followed them and waited outside the room in case I could be of help. I dug in my purse for a business card and wrote my home phone number on the back and held it in my hand. It was almost an hour before she appeared again. I walked up to her and said, "Mrs. Chamberlain, I'm so sorry. I really admired your daughter, and I want to be of help in any way I can."

She was staring at the floor now.

I could see her hands were trembling, and, by some sort of sympathetic vibration, I began to tremble, too. I felt as if the orderly world I had known and depended upon only a few hours before had fallen away like a snow mass in an avalanche. "Can I take you somewhere, Mrs. Chamberlain?" I finally asked.

She shook her head. "I would like a glass of water, please," she said then.

I was extremely grateful to be asked to be of assistance to her in some small way. "Here, please, sit here," I said. The chair I had pulled from the nurses' station for Lou was still sitting outside Constance's room. "I'll be right back."

I went over to the nurse at the front desk and asked for a glass of water. Then, paper cup in hand, I hurried back to Mrs. Chamberlain. She drank the water slowly. "If only her father were here, but . . ." She lowered her head. "What difference would it make."

She looked up at me.

I awkwardly handed her my card. "My home phone number is on the back. Please call me if you need anything."

"Thank you," she said.

As I tried to decide what to do next, I saw a tall, thin couple, youngish looking but probably in their late forties, hurrying toward Mrs. Chamberlain. The woman embraced her and tears sprang to Mrs. Chamberlain's eyes for the first time.

I suddenly felt like an intruder, and backed away from the three of them and left the hospital.

·   ·   ·

Two days later Mrs. Chamberlain called my office and told me a memorial service was going to be held at the Brick Presbyterian Church on Park Avenue at Ninety-first Street for Constance's

New York friends. For some reason I couldn't quite put my finger on, this greatly surprised me. After putting the receiver back in its cradle, I sat there for a while staring at the notepad with the information I had written down—Brick Presbyterian Church, Wednesday, 2:00 P.M. Then it occurred to me that I had mistakenly assumed that Constance was largely friendless. She herself had told me that day at the Waldorf that she had no one she could really confide in, so I naturally thought . . . I tapped my pen on top of my doodle-strewn desk blotter. "How little I really knew her," I thought, and yet I felt as if I'd lost someone very close to me, someone I had known for years and years.

There were more people at the memorial service than I had expected.

The windows of the redbrick neo-Georgian church, one of the most famous in New York, filtered the afternoon sun through semiopaque Colonial glass. An intricately patterned wrought-iron pulpit sat on the left side of the chancel, and two large vases of white roses—Constance's favorite flower—flanked a small shiny gold cross on the altar. Three little golden, winged cherubim stared down at the mourners from the ceiling overhead. I kept looking around the pews for Lou, but I couldn't find him. My eyes were drawn again and again to the red doors at the back of the church, expecting at any moment his dark-suited figure to appear, but I saw only strangers, and I felt that familiar discomfort that comes from being without friends or acquaintances in a room full of people. I knew that if I could just catch sight of his tan features for even a moment, I would feel much less alone. Finally, Matt came in and sat down next to me and alleviated considerably my growing sense of isolation.

"Is he here?" he asked. I shook my head. "Son of a . . ." he said under his breath before I grabbed his arm and reminded him where we were.

The Reverend Dieter Dreifaldt performed the service. He was a fair-skinned man of perhaps sixty with pencil-thin lips and snowy white hair, who possessed a deep baritone voice that resonated throughout the sanctuary and evoked memories of New England orators of days long past. He had known Constance as a child when she lived in Lake Forest and attended the First Presbyterian Church with her parents, he said. He had been the minister there before moving to New York.

"Constance used to sit in the front row and listen to my sermons with an intensity that most ministers only dream of from their parishioners," he began. He looked down to the spot where she would have been. "I didn't see her as often in New York. She told me she'd become skeptical of doctrine of any kind, especially church doctrine. Occasionally, though, I'd be standing up here, and I'd look down and she'd be sitting there watching me, seeing if I had anything interesting to say. I always knew when I'd hit the mark because she would linger after the service to discuss some aspect of the sermon. If I hadn't delivered, I wouldn't see her."

Knowing smiles momentarily lit up the faces of the assembled mourners.

Dr. Dreifaldt looked intently out over the crowded pews. I noticed his pale white hands rigidly clutching the sides of the lectern.

"She told me once that it was the poetry of the Bible that she admired most. She said it was the poetry in the Bible that gave it meaning. The poetry of thought, as well as the poetry of words. She said it was largely a language of symbol and metaphor that few people could truly understand. She said it took her a long time to understand it."

Dr. Dreifaldt paused again as if he were trying to communicate some larger meaning here.

"But God's message got through to our young, beautiful Constance. She may have been skeptical of doctrine, but she believed in the Word. 'I am the way, the truth, and the life.' She knew what that meant. She knew the love of the Lord and of Jesus Christ, our hope and our redeemer."

I smiled at Dr. Dreifaldt's presumptuousness. I knew very well that Constance was not the type to project her spiritual impulses out there, as it were, on Jesus Christ, or the Virgin Mary, or the cross, or the Holy Ghost. She was too smart for that; she didn't need it. She knew that all authentic religious experiences are personal experiences. They don't come from above; they can't be appropriated, and they have nothing to do with the church. When Jesus said, "The kingdom of God is within you," he meant it, and that was where Constance looked for it. There and nowhere else.

Dr. Dreifaldt's lower lip began to quiver, and he looked deep into his notes as he tried to regain his composure. "What does it mean when a vibrant young person is taken from us unexpectedly? What sense can we make of it? How can God help us to deal with our sorrow and our disbelief? It says in . . ."

Constance was right, I thought, the mystery of the Bible is in its poetry. In its ability to evoke other worlds. That was the mystery of all poetry. It was a mystery that, because she had experienced it directly, provided her with a presumption of eternity that I was quite sure was the envy of this minister. Her understanding of the spiritual world had nothing to do with faith. She didn't need faith. She'd experienced the divine directly.

I felt, as I listened to Dr. Dreifaldt's eulogy, that he had been searching his whole life for this same kind of certainty, but hadn't found it yet. I'd heard other ministers at funerals and Christmas services who sounded very much like him. Ministers who had become ministers because they were looking for something. Men, usually, who had chosen a path they'd hoped would lead to understanding and salvation, but instead led only to more uncertainty and wonder, more dead ends and unanswerable questions.

By the time Dr. Dreifaldt finished, a profound silence had enveloped the assembled mourners. Everyone was staring at the black-robed figure in the pulpit with rapt attention as he slowly removed his reading glasses.

The focus that he demanded stemmed, however, less from what he was saying and more from the way he was saying it. His eyes were damp throughout and his voice was almost choking with grief. It was hard to believe, but I would have sworn that he was a little bit in love with Constance—even in her death. "I will always think of *my* Constance as God's special gift to the world," he said in closing. "Let us pray." We bowed our heads; then, as if on cue, a cloud passed over the bright winter sun and the church darkened.

The heightened, dreamlike atmosphere in that old church stayed with me for a long time.

When I got home that evening, I sat down on my bed and took the poems out of the binder Constance had given me. I was about to begin sorting through them when I remembered what she had said about Sylvia Plath's poems and the fact that they had not, after her death, been published in the order in which she had intended them to be read. I broke into a cold sweat as I realized that I had almost lost the only order she had ever given me for these poems, if indeed she had arranged them in any sort of specific order. I carefully put them back in the binder and moved over to my desk and began to write out a title list duplicating the order in the binder.

As I read through them, my belief in her work grew. They fulfilled my one criterion for all art—they were interesting. They broke rules and they weren't perfect, but in almost every poem there was at least one line that promised to stay in my memory. That was much more than I could say for most of the manuscripts that found their way onto my desk every day.

I had hoped before the accident that as I worked with Constance, I would slowly come to understand her. Now that she was gone, I had to search for her in the poetry she had left behind. It was all I had, and with eternity between us now to provide a deeper level of objectivity, I began to go through her work with fresh eyes. And as I read, I began to notice, the way you slowly notice that a room has become darker and darker with the fading sun, that my view of her had not been exactly accurate. Without realizing it, I had imposed a very old image on a unique person. I hadn't meant to do it. I'd even actively campaigned against it, but I had done it all the same. Seeing this was humbling because I have always prided myself on being an open-minded, forward-thinking kind of person.

Constance was a beautiful woman, physically, spiritually, and intellectually, and because of this I had never seriously entertained the thought that she might be suffering. The evidence was right there in front of me all along, in her reticence, her wandering eyes, her silences, and most especially in her poetry, but some part of me couldn't really believe it. The sheer force of her presence, her sparkling mind and quiet glamour, shunted aside all deeper reflection. It was so easy when you were talking to her to get lost in her thoughts and ideas and your own reactions to them—the deep internal epiphanies and intuitive sparks of recognition—that seeing her clearly became nearly impossible, if it was thought about at all.

I wondered if she knew this, if she had discovered somewhere along the line that her intelligence, charm, and physical attractiveness could be used to keep people at a distance, while creating the illusion that they were inside the palace gates speaking to the real person. That was the impression she had given me that day at the Waldorf. I'd felt like a privileged confidante, but had I been? What had she told me after all? Nothing, really, about herself. Nothing about her own feelings beyond the fact that she was in love with a man named Lou Ellis, who just happened to be one of the most famous and influential men in the city. With information like this laid at your feet, it was hard to think about anything else.

But now I began to. I tried as hard as I could to filter out all the distracting romantic fantasies I had projected onto her life.

She was not a princess locked up in a castle tower perfecting her art, or a heroine in a tragic love story. She was a writer who had immersed herself in the world around her and had worked very hard to translate what she saw and experienced into words and images that would resonate in other people's imaginations. As she wrote in one of her poems:

> I've been to the far reaches of this country
> And examined the earth on my knees.
>
> I've explored many people—
> All those internal clocks ticking inside.
>
> I dismantled them all.
> So when you're imagining me,
>
> I wouldn't be imagining castles.
> You'll have to imagine
>
> All those other things
> You feared.
>
> No one
> Was protecting me.

As I read through her work, the belief grew in me that she was speaking directly to me through her poems. I think all readers feel this way when they fall in love with a writer's work, and I actively fostered the illusion in myself by creating elaborate theories that explained where the poems came from. As I later discovered, some of my theories turned out to be true—in particular, the belief I had that a great deal of the quiet, tightly held pain that ran through her poetry like an underground stream sprang from her relationship with her father. As she wrote in the following poem, entitled "Belladonna":

> The poison is still in me,
> My love.
> I can't quite make out
> What you're asking for—
> I have no beauty.
> My heart is aching.
> I feel no love.
> My mind is laced with substances
> You could trace.
> A patient doctor
> Would be able to discover what is wrong.
> It was those wild berries I ate
> While the bells in the chapel bonged.
> They made me feel like a child again
> Who has no business reaching out for love.
> They were as familiar as the belladonnas
> My father grew at our front door.
> They had the same blue-purple, dull red color
> That speaks to my core.
> They were comfortable, familiar.
> They gave me nothing to hope for.
> They were poisonous in the appetite

They gave me for beauty—
It's easy to let night fall
When you find yourself at the threshold
Of some place you've never been before.

I never heard from Lou again, which surprised me. I kept expecting him to contact me, but the anticipated telephone call
never came. Maybe he felt guilty; maybe he wanted to slip back
into his old, familiar life with as little fuss as possible; maybe he
was afraid to face the possibility that his own insecurities and
uncertainties had played a part in her death. Whatever his reasons were, I was certain they must have been influenced by the
headlines that filled the New York tabloids: LOU ELLIS'S SHOCKING
DOUBLE LIFE, THE BIGGER THEY COME . . . , HYPOCRITE'S OATH, JUDG-
MENT DAY, LOU ELLIS'S BOOK OF REVELATIONS. In all of these stories, Constance was completely unrecognizable to me. It was as
if a diamond capable of refracting a thousand suns had been reduced to a piece of coal, and it left me with a nagging sense of
injustice and an irksome anger that I found impossible to sub-
due. I tried to convince myself that it was simply the way of
things, but that didn't sit well with my notion of fairness. A desire for retribution was growing in me, and I began casting
about for something to do on her behalf. Getting her into print
was the most obvious possibility. But it was a possibility with
pretty long odds. She was a poet, after all, not a romance novelist or a mystery writer. It wasn't going to be easy to convince the
powers that be that a book of poems by a dead poet, even a dead
poet with a scandalous past, was going to be a good investment.
Would people be able to see past the notoriety to the inherent

value of the work, even if I could get a book published? Was there a market for the kinds of poems she had written, especially the longer ones? Could I make people see in her work what I saw in it? Did I really have the time and energy to try? I kept asking myself these types of questions.

Then I came into my office one morning and found a newspaper clipping on my chair with a Post-it note stuck on it that read:

Morgan,

I believe this is the first poem that Constance gave you. I remember you let me read it. I found this in the *Post*.

Linda

I knew my assistant, Linda, had been following the story in the tabloids even more closely than I had—the newspapers were always sticking out of her tote bag when she came in each morning.

I examined the clipping. It was, indeed, Constance's poem "A Dialogue in Silence." How it had gotten into the hands of the *Post* would remain a mystery to me. I figured the poem must have gotten into circulation through a friend or acquaintance. I smiled at the peculiarity of seeing a poem like this in a newspaper like the *Post*. But then it occurred to me that seeing a poem printed in any newspaper anywhere nowadays would be strange.

After the publication of Constance's poem, the story gained new life. It genuinely touched a number of readers, who wrote letters to the paper asking about the author. They wanted to know more about her and whether she had published other poems, or a book of poems, and what the title was and where they could buy it. I started thinking about the publication of Edgar Allan Poe's "The Raven" in a New York newspaper some 150 years before. The appearance of this one poem had brought Poe the recognition he'd been craving for years. It made his name. It seemed improbable that it could happen this way today, but it *was* happening.

People clipped the poem out of the paper and stuck it on their bulletin boards and refrigerators, and Cynthia Zeck, a distinguished New York stage actress, even did a reading on National Public Radio. Then one of the more cantankerous literary critics at *The New York Times,* Christian Bent, used the poem as a centerpiece for an article on the difficulties and barriers that talented writers often face in the current commercial market. "There is something seriously wrong in publishing today," he wrote, "if a work of such music and beauty cannot find a place in the plethora of literary magazines that dot our landscape. Do we all have tin ears? Have we completely lost touch with what constitutes poetry?" In no time, I found myself sitting on what I was sure was a little gold mine, and I went in, armed with all the newspaper clippings, to talk to Matt about putting together a book of her poems.

"You'd have to get permission from her mother, assuming she's the executor of her estate," he said.

"I know. I could call her."

"Why don't you go out there?"

"To Illinois?"

"Why not? Mrs. Chamberlain loved her daughter very much. She believed in her. You should be able to convince her."

"Okay," I said, thrilled by this unqualified show of support. "I'll go, then." I got up to leave. "Thank you," I said.

He waved my gratitude away.

When I got to the door, I turned around.

"Matt."

He looked up.

"Do you think it's all luck, or do you think fate has anything to do with the way things turn out? I mean, if a writer or an artist is meant to be known, do you think they will be known, no matter what?" I wouldn't normally have posed a question like this to Matt. He wasn't someone whose mind ran toward philosophical speculation, but it had been on my mind for a while, and I didn't have anyone else to ask—at least, not anyone who would understand why I was asking.

He gazed at the papers on his desk for a moment, then at me. "Yes," he said. "If they're meant to be known, I think they will be."

"It's nice to look at things that way, isn't it?" I said, thinking about how easy it would have been for a poet like Constance to have disappeared into the ether. "It makes you feel as if the world makes sense, even when it doesn't."

He nodded. "Yes, it does."

We smiled at each other then, and for a moment, like a spaceship reentering the earth's atmosphere, a certain distance that had arisen between us over the years closed considerably.

·   ·   ·

Two days later, I was sitting in Mrs. Chamberlain's stately living room. She still lived in Lake Forest in a white two-story black-shuttered Colonial that sat back from the street like an imposing monarch. The house was just as I had imagined it would be on the plane ride—polished wood floors, rose-patterned damask-upholstered furniture, white ceiling molding. On a baby grand piano in the corner sat a studio portrait of Constance. And across from me on the living room sofa sat Mrs. Chamberlain. She was wearing a black turtleneck sweater and gray wool slacks.

"She was protecting *him*, not me. She told me everything. We were as close as a mother and daughter could be." We were talking about Constance's relationship with Lou—something Mrs. Chamberlain was explaining to me had not been a secret to her, despite what Lou might have thought.

"I didn't know that," I said. "I mean, I didn't know that you knew. We never really discussed it. Not that we would have, but . . ."

"It's fine," she said, mercifully relieving me of my self-consciousness. "She used to tell me that people told her she was mysterious. Maybe she was. She used to take long walks around this neighborhood. You see we have sidewalks here in the Midwest. That was how she worked out her problems." Mrs. Chamberlain smiled thoughtfully. "If she had a stomachache, she'd drag herself out of bed and take a three-mile walk. She thought of it as a kind of physical and emotional cure-all."

We both smiled now, and then the expression on Mrs. Chamberlain's face grew very grave. She stared out the window at a group of children building a snowman in the yard across the street. "I miss her."

I didn't know what to say except to tell her how sorry I was and how much I missed her daughter, too.

"It's going to take time," I told her, thinking of the many cold winter nights I had spent sitting in my apartment, staring out the window after my husband died.

"I know." She folded her hands in her lap. "Now, you said you had something you wanted to talk to me about."

"Yes. I imagine you've heard about the interest and curiosity Constance's 'A Dialogue in Silence' has generated in New York?"

"Yes, I have," she said. "Her aunt and uncle live in Manhattan. I've heard all about it."

"It's a very strange thing, Mrs. Chamberlain, what has happened with that poem. It was the first poem she sent me. I've always loved it."

"There's a line in that poem that has meant a lot to me."

"What line is that?" I asked.

" 'The attraction bled.' "

" 'The attraction bled'?"

"Constance said I understood that line better than she did. That was often the case. I would make her aware of things in her work that she'd never considered before."

"That must have been enlightening for her."

"I think it was. She was curious about what other people saw in her work. Whether she agreed with what they saw, I don't know. But she was always curious."

I thought of asking Mrs. Chamberlain what the line meant to her, but then I figured that if she wanted to tell me, she would, and when she didn't, I moved on.

"I spoke with our editor in chief, Matt Peabody. He said he knew you."

"Yes, he was a college friend of Constance's."

"He's very supportive of her work, and we, Peabody & Simms, would like to publish a book of her poems."

Mrs. Chamberlain looked at me steadily. I could not tell at first what her reaction was, and I feared I had not presented the idea properly. This fear grew to a certainty when she drew up her spine and said, sharply, "Why should I condone the production of a book of poems based on the notoriety of my dead daughter?"

"Because they are beautiful poems, and because there is so little beauty in the world right now. Constance said that she never wrote her poetry for her own amusement but because she felt compelled to communicate something of the world that she felt only she could see. She told me this once."

"I'm sorry," she apologized, the steely look in her eyes softening. "I didn't mean to snap at you. I get very angry."

"Of course," I said. "I can imagine. I mean . . . I can't imagine, but it is certainly understandable. It's just that . . ." Words were failing me when I needed them most, and I could feel my heart dropping. I took a breath and tried to start again. "I just feel strongly, Mrs. Chamberlain, that we have a very rare opportunity right now to bring recognition to Constance's poetry, and I want to seize that opportunity for her sake."

"Why?"

"Because she deserves it."

Mrs. Chamberlain looked down at her hands. "Yes, she does." Then, after a brief silence, she looked up and gazed at the

children across the street again. They were sticking black char-
coal eyes and a carrot nose in their lopsided snowman and wrap-
ping an old jacket around his shoulders so he wouldn't get cold.
"I want to show you something," she said, and walked over and
opened the bottom drawer of an antique secretary in the corner
of the room. She came back with a folder and took out a thin
sheet of pink paper with a lot of marks and notes on it. "This is
Constance's third-grade report card. Look at what her teacher
wrote."

I took the paper and read what a "delight" Constance was to
have in class, and how "fascinated" the teacher was by her "ma-
ture behavior and attitude," and—what I knew Mrs. Chamberlain wanted me to read—that "Constance shows an unusual
interest in poetry and literature."

I looked up. "So it showed even then?"

"Her favorite book from the time she could read was *A
Child's Book of Poems.*"

"I remember that book," I said. "It was beautifully illus-
trated."

"It was," Mrs. Chamberlain said tearfully.

"I've always thought of talent as something inborn," I told
her, "as a kind of gift from God."

"But it has to be developed. Talent alone is never enough.
Constance was a hard worker." Mrs. Chamberlain's evocation of
the work ethic marked her indubitably as a midwesterner.

She put the report card back in the folder. Then she got up
and returned the folder to the bottom drawer of the secretary. I
could tell by her slow, measured pace that she was thinking. By
the time she sat down again, there was a look of resignation on

her face. "You may put together a book of her poems, Morgan, but I would like to have final approval."

"That's fine," I said. "You'll have final approval. We'll work on it together."

A sad, wistful smile played at the corners of her mouth and then fluttered away.

"I've forgotten how to be happy," she said, and then she shook her head as if she were trying to push something dark and restless from her thoughts.

I reached out and touched her arm in a vain attempt to provide some comfort.

"I have an idea," she said then. "Why don't you stay here tonight? I'll put you in Constance's old room. We can talk further then, and you won't have to stay in a cold, unfriendly hotel room."

"I don't want to put you out."

"No, you wouldn't be. I insist. Is your bag in the car?"

I said it was.

"Then it's decided."

·   ·   ·

Mrs. Chamberlain opened the door to Constance's room, which still retained the remnants of her girlhood—a white lace canopy bed, a patchwork pillow Mrs. Chamberlain said Constance had made in high school, and a statue of a horse jumping over a stone wall that sat on her dresser. "I've been going through her papers," she said, looking at the pile of folders on her desk. She walked over and began searching for something. "There was one folder in here of essays she wrote that you might be interested in looking through. Here it is." She set it on the chair. "I'll let you relax from your trip. Come down whenever you're ready, and we'll go to dinner."

.   .   .

We went to a restaurant in Lake Forest called the Deer Path Inn, an impressive pile of half timbers, stucco, and stone that reminded me of an English manor house. "We stayed here for two weeks when we first came to Lake Forest, while we were still moving in," Mrs. Chamberlain explained. She gazed around the room as if she expected Constance to walk in at any moment. "Constance was about to start high school when we came here. She was not happy about that move. She wanted to stay in Los Angeles. She thought it was too cold here and said she hated the way all the boys and girls dressed exactly the same—in Levi's, alligator shirts, and Docksiders—'the ugliest shoes on earth,' she used to call them. She never owned a pair."

"She was very feminine," I said, thinking back on her many eye-catching outfits. "I admired her style."

"She liked being a girl and she was very feminine, but she was a good athlete too. When she was five I took her to the Y for swimming lessons. She was in a class with all boys. She was the best swimmer in the group and the only one who would jump off the diving board. She was very brave."

I smiled and looked around the room. "It's very nice." White damask tablecloths, Chippendale chairs, and Wedgwood blue walls evoked the feeling of a genteel country estate. "I like the chandeliers." Hanging like giant gold crowns from the crossbeam overhead, they suffused the room with a warm glow.

Mrs. Chamberlain took in the room appreciatively. "It is nice, isn't it? It's very Old World, a real Anglo-heaven."

I started to laugh.

She shrugged. "Well, it is. Constance told me that F. Scott Fitzgerald once called Lake Forest 'the most glamorous place in the world.' I've always found that hard to believe. It's a lovely town, but glamorous? It's not glamorous. New York is glamorous. Lake Forest is quaint."

As I listened to her tell me a bit of the history of the town she made her home, an overwhelming feeling of déjà vu swept over me. She sounded so much like Constance it was disconcerting, and I began to find it difficult to concentrate on what she was actually saying. I could see at once where her daughter had gotten her curiosity and her intelligence. She spoke in the same intricately patterned paragraphs that had so characterized Constance's conversations. The manners, the politeness, and the measured reactions were all there, too. No wonder they had been close, I thought; they were so much alike.

It was when I realized this that the full weight of her loss came home to me. I thought losing Constance must have been for Mrs. Chamberlain like losing her own reflection, and my heart went out to her.

"So, what would you like?" she said. I opened the menu lying on the table in front of me. The dinner fare was as sumptuous as the surroundings: slow-roasted Atlantic salmon, seared sea bass with "forbidden" black rice, marinated grilled rack of Colorado lamb.

When our waiter came to take our order, Mrs. Chamberlain asked him, very innocently, why the rice was forbidden.

He peered over her shoulder at the menu. "I don't know, Ma'am. Would you like me to check with the chef?"

"No, that won't be necessary," she said. "I was just curious. It sounds so intriguing."

"I can assure you it is an exquisite dish," he told her in a slightly affected English accent.

After he left with our order, we sat back and began to talk about our new project. I could tell that Mrs. Chamberlain loved talking about her daughter's work. I think she sensed, as I did, that there was the opportunity for some small measure of redemption in the act of publishing Constance's poetry.

"How much of her work have you read?" she asked me.

"She gave me a binder of her poems. I counted them the other day. There were exactly one hundred."

"That's less than a third of what she wrote," she said.

"I'd be interested to read the rest of them," I told her. "Did she regularly show you her work?"

"Oh, yes. I loved her poetry. She knew that. I would read certain poems over and over again."

I asked which ones were her favorites.

"There are many. 'A Dialogue in Silence' will always be special to me. That was her breakthrough poem. I'm particularly fond of 'The Mutual Muse' and 'Madeline's Magical Will.' "

"I haven't read the last one you mentioned." I asked her what it was about.

"It's a fairy tale in a way," she said. "At least, that's what she told me after she wrote it. It's about a young woman locked in a dungeon with only books for companions. Eventually, she's released and, after finding her own poetic voice, agrees to marry."

The fairy-tale aspect of the poem interested me considerably because I knew it was a difficult form to work in. For a fairy tale to succeed, it must enchant, and to enchant, it must cast a very deep spell, and casting spells is one of the most mysterious aspects of artistic creation. Nobody has ever really been able to tell somebody else how to do it. The oft-repeated admonition to "be yourself" probably comes closest to the mark, but for most people, being oneself is no small task. It's an experience akin to climbing Mount Everest in the middle of a blizzard.

Mrs. Chamberlain studied me for a moment. "She told me it was the most autobiographical poem she'd ever written. She said it was her favorite."

"Maybe I can read it when we get back to the house," I suggested.

"Yes, of course," she said. "I'll find it for you." She began absently tapping her finger on top of the table as if she were sending a telegram. "I have another poem with me that you probably haven't seen," she said. I watched as she took a leather wallet from her handbag and pulled out a small piece of paper folded into a little slot behind her credit cards.

She smoothed out the creases and laid it in front of me.

"That poem was a present. She gave it to me on my fiftieth birthday."

A SACRIFICE MY MOTHER MADE

You walked in an apparition all your own.
The moonlight took you back to your girlhood;
Your hair turned black.

I saw who my mother once was.
It was all before me and my first breath.
The promise of a life
Not yet filled.
Your dress was the color
Of pink rose petals and yellow daffodils.
I knew then
That something was lost
When I was born.
Youth drew away
As you became full of silent disclosures,
Or maybe it was all the love you gave.
I saw you in the moonlight.
You walked differently,
As if you had no reason to turn back.

"She said it was a thank-you from her to me for giving birth to her. I told her she didn't have to thank me, but she said she did. She said to me, 'I just want you to know that I understand. I do.' 'Understand what?' I asked. 'I understand that a mother sacrifices a lot when she has a child,' she said. I protested, but I could tell she was very sure of this. I think what she was trying to say was that she didn't want me to feel guilty about mistakes I made when she was young, because I did make mistakes."

"But all parents make mistakes," I said.

She smiled. "That's what she used to say to me." She began to put the poem back in her wallet.

I hesitated and then said, "May I have a copy?"

She froze for a moment and that sinking feeling of having

overstepped my bounds flooded through me again. "Let me think about it, Morgan, I . . ."

"Of course," I said. "You may want to keep it for yourself. She wrote it, after all, for you."

She put her purse under the table again. Then she clasped her hands together and gazed out the mullioned windows at a long row of arching elms. "This inn is almost seventy years old. There are two elderly ladies who have lived in this hotel for over thirty years. Can you imagine that?"

I said I couldn't.

Our waiter arrived with our salads, and as I watched him lay them in front of us, I decided to broach a topic that had been in the back of my mind since that day at the Waldorf when Constance first told me about her relationship with Lou.

"Mrs. Chamberlain," I began.

"Please, call me Louise."

"Louise, then. Constance told me in some detail about her relationship with Lou, but what she told me had much more to do with him than with her. She barely touched on her own history, but she left hardly anything of his side of the story unexamined. And I was just wondering what you think drew her to him. I mean, he was so much . . ."

"So much older?"

"Yes."

"I know."

"I only ask because, as you obviously know, she was very beautiful. She could have, it seems to me, found someone . . . anyone . . ."

"Free and her own age?"

"Yes."

"She could have. I don't think she meant to fall in love with Lou. I think he took her by surprise. She had things she wanted to accomplish before she got married and settled down. To be honest, she had some ambivalence toward the whole institution of marriage. I'm afraid her father and I did not set a great example for her. We had a difficult marriage, and then, of course, there was the suicide."

"I'm sorry, Mrs. Chamberlain—I mean, Louise," I said, "but I thought your husband had a heart attack."

"A heart attack? No, it wasn't a heart attack."

"But, I thought . . . Matt told me."

Mrs. Chamberlain lowered her head. "I don't think Constance wanted anyone to know what he'd done. Her father shot himself in the basement one afternoon when I was at the grocery store," she said. "Of course, everyone around here knew, but she didn't want people at school to know. She took his death very personally. I could never seem to make her understand that it wasn't her fault."

"Of course it wasn't. It couldn't have been," I said.

"I know, but she didn't see it that way, at least not initially. She felt that she should have paid more attention to him, even though he paid almost no attention to her. She thought maybe if she'd been a boy, he would have liked her more. Over the past few years she'd begun to write about her father—in an indirect fashion, of course—and I could see she was beginning to find some peace with him. There is one poem she wrote about him that just takes my breath away every time I read it."

"What is it called?"

" 'The Forest Disagrees.' "

"I haven't read that one," I said.

"It's in the pile of folders I left for you upstairs."

"I'll pay special attention to it," I promised. Then I sat there staring at my silverware as I tried to integrate this calamitous loss into my understanding of her life. "Louise," I finally said, with a feeling of bottomless curiosity. "What was her father like?"

"He was extremely reserved," she said. "He never, under any conditions, spoke about his true feelings. He was expert at talking around things, at obfuscation. It was maddening at times. The obvious answer, then, to your earlier question about why she chose Lou might be that she had a father complex of some sort, but I think that, if that played a part at all, it was only a small part. Lou really wasn't anything like her father. Her father was distant and busy and always preoccupied with his work. He never *saw* her. Lou was a busy man, of course, but he was there for her as much as he possibly could be, considering the circumstances. And I can't deny the fact that he did love her. Hopelessly." She sighed. "I'm afraid Lou and I had one thing in common. We relied on her a great deal. She told me Lou used to call her and say, 'I need my Constance fix.' If he couldn't speak to her for three days, he would begin to go crazy. I used to do the same thing. I used to use exactly the same words—my Constance fix. She was always there for me, even as a little girl. She had a way of seeing things, of making the essence of things shine through. I'd speak to her, my mind would clear, and I would finally be able to distinguish what was true and what was false. She did the same for him. His life was so full of compromises and lies that he couldn't see straight sometimes. But when he was with her, the clouds parted, his vision sharpened, and he could be honest with himself. That's why he could never let her go, despite the unfairness of the situation. It would have been like separating his soul from his body."

"I went to dinner with them," I told her. "Just a week or so before the accident. I could tell he loved her, but there was something in him that was intractable. Something that held him to the past, just as Constance said. But I don't think even he knew what it was. Why would a man with so much power and money choose to stay in a cold, unfulfilling, sexless marriage when he could have been with a beautiful young woman who was madly in love with him? There had to be something holding him back."

"Fear," she said without hesitation.

I looked at her.

"Fear. I spent over twenty years in an unhappy marriage because of it. I told myself, of course, that I was doing it for Constance—for my child. It's very noble to think that way. It makes you feel like a martyr. But that wasn't why I stayed. And believe me, staying didn't help Constance at all. Pretending to be happy is a far cry from being happy. I stayed because I was afraid. I couldn't conceive of any other life besides the life I had. You could chalk it up to a lack of imagination, I suppose. For a long time I chose to cast a blind eye on the emptiness in my life, at the lack of a real connection with my husband, never grasping what the repercussions of that choice would be. You see, Constance was trying to do with Lou what she had done with me all those years. She was trying to make him see things. She was repeating the past, her own past. She was again on the outside of a marriage looking in, her face pressed against the glass, watching, waiting, hoping." She took a sip of her wine, and I could tell that her hand was trembling. She set down her glass awkwardly. "The roots of Lou's life were rotten, but he could not dig them up and plant new ones. Did you know that I never received even a condolence card from him?"

"No, I didn't know that," I answered.

There was a long silence then until Mrs. Chamberlain said, "It isn't going to bring her back, you know. Talking like this. Talking about him. I've already gone over it so many times in my head. I'm becoming sick from it. Let's talk more about her poems. Tell me your ideas for the book. Have you thought of a title?"

I told her I wanted to call it "A Dialogue in Silence." She thought for a moment, then said she liked that idea very much.

· · ·

That night I sat at Constance's old desk reading through the folders of poems and essays Mrs. Chamberlain had laid out for me. The first one I looked for was the one Mrs. Chamberlain had mentioned at dinner—Constance's poem about her father.

THE FOREST DISAGREES

> It's hard to become a stranger,
> But somewhere deep within the forest
> You passed out of me.
> You traveled like a ghost

Among the trees.
For years you kept coming after me,
Trying to turn me back into
What I no longer wanted to be.
The animals knew this;
They tried to intervene.
Owls screeched.
Snakes bit at your heels regularly.
You paid them no heed.
You spoke of love,
But I had no desire
To bring you back to me.

I reread the poem four or five times. I wondered if Constance had actually told Mrs. Chamberlain that this poem was about her father or if Mrs. Chamberlain simply assumed that that was what it was about. It could have been about so many things—her father, Lou, her own past.

I also paid special attention to "Madeline's Magical Will"—the poem Constance thought of as a fairy tale.

It began, as so many of her poems began, with deceptive simplicity.

It is spring
And the sun is full in the sky.
The trees are unfolding their leaves,
And the rosebuds are anxious to show what they
    can do.
Winter ended
Without Madeline ever expecting it to.

The poem told the story of a young woman, a sort of princess-poet in the making, and her love affair with books and reading, a love affair as rapturous and all-consuming, as joyous and disillusioning, as any other. The heroine, Madeline, becomes obsessed with the stories of "the gods and the troubadours" and finds herself enveloped "in forms that she had had no part in molding." What saves her, in the end, is her ability to tell her own story, something Constance had been working on when she died.

The poem was a small marvel, and as I studied it, I looked for the story within the story. It wasn't immediately obvious, even to my practiced eyes, but it could be seen. I just had to read it enough times, as it were, for the metaphorical distractions to fall away and the heart of the writer to appear. She'd written a story that took place in a castle with a prince and a library dungeon, a place where, when things weren't going well, "roses gave way to weeds. / Cats began meowing, / And dogs turned gradually mean." In other words, a magical place whose surroundings mimicked the mental state of its inhabitants. A world sensitive enough to register the fact that "part of her was alive / To the part of her that was dead."

After she spends three years in isolated reading and studying, the prince comes to retrieve her from her library dungeon, and finds her in a much-altered state. She is a young lady now to her imagination "utterly wed," and she pays no attention to him. She wanders meditatively through the castle grounds, working on her writing and feeling trapped in the middle of "other people's symphonies." Confused, but still in love, the prince waits patiently for her to come back to herself while busying himself with his princely duties.

I knew that, like Madeline, Constance had closed herself off from the world for many years to read and study. I also knew that she had met a prince, Lou, who was patient enough to allow her to develop at her own pace, who didn't push her into being something she wasn't, who loved her beyond questioning. I also suspected that, as with Madeline, the more Constance looked within, the colder she felt. And, finally, I knew that, like her heroine, Constance had been dependent on poetry and the beauty of words.

I also sensed, though, that by the end of the poem Madeline had ascended to a level of understanding that Constance had never fully attained: a perfect example of an artist's work transcending her own powers of comprehension. As Constance wrote about her wiser, more fortunate alter ego:

> Her words erupted.
> Her nights grew bolder.
> Madeline after four years
> Felt the beauty of growing older.

> Experience braided itself into her long blond hair—
> She had beauty,
> Talent,
> Love,
> And now a royal air.

> The Prince kissed her
> And began to speak about all they would share.
> She listened
> And prepared for a wedding of great fanfare.

This part of her life had resumed.
But still, sometimes,
When she sees her children so happy and free,
She remembers what she went through
On those long, deceptively quiet afternoons
When it was so hard to see.

Constance didn't live to see "her children so happy and free" as her character Madeline did, and she never arrived at a place where she could look back and remember "when it was so hard to see." But if she had lived, I was sure, in time she would have reached this place that her imagination had so carefully prepared for her.

As in "Madeline's Magical Will," her writing always bore this imprint of transformation. It was never strictly confessional. "When you write a poem," Constance told me once, "you reveal everything and nothing." I think that's why she fell in love with poetry, because she could say things in a poem that she would never have been able to say in "real life." The metaphorical, suggestive, impressionistic nature of poetry provided her with a certain level of protection, while at the same time it provided her with a channel for the expression of her emotions. Perhaps that was why her interest and love of the art form surfaced so early.

I believe that poetry, by and large, finds its life source in suppressed emotions. A poet is to me a volcano that occasionally erupts in a lava flow of language. The words and emotions issue forth from a fissure in the poet's psyche simply because they have nowhere else to go. It is all about, as Emily Dickinson said, a soul working at a *"White Heat."*

This is what I saw taking place in Constance's poetry. From what I had been able to piece together about her life, it was obvious that she had not grown up in an atmosphere conducive to self-expression. She had clearly put her own youthful desires aside in order to support her mother, who had depended on her in lieu of a loving husband. I had known many writers who had grown up in similar circumstances. It's often the paucity of emotional support in childhood that shapes an artist. Indeed, it is the reason most people become artists—to fill this void. Constance was no exception. Her writing was, I believe, for her, a life-sustaining gift, and this may have accounted for her unwillingness to abandon poetry, even temporarily, to write a novel.

"I love castles," she wrote, with a directness common to many of her poems:

> They speak to my nature—
> Elaborate and dark.
> They used to light candles in these places at night,
> But still you could barely see.
> Those walls were built for protection.
> I feel safe having those walls around me.

It was after midnight when I finally stopped reading. After pacing back and forth for a while, I sat down in the armchair next to Constance's window. The disappointment of never being able to speak with her again was palpable, especially because I had a lot of things I wanted to talk with her about. I wanted to know if my conclusions about her were true, if I had understood her correctly. I wanted to know what she had been referring to when she wrote, "The color of my roses grew red. Wondrous potentialities filled my head." I wanted to know what her plans were and which poems she would have chosen for the book. And most of all, I wanted to tell her that her poetry had had a profound influence on my life.

When I finally turned out the light, after indulging for a while in thoughts of what might have been, it was almost one in the morning, and it was snowing outside.

10

I took more care editing this book than any other. I was meticulous about the layout, the typeface, and especially the dust
jacket. I even suggested an artist named Francesco Cougar, a
friend of my husband's, to design the cover. In the center of
Francesco's painting was a portrait of a modern-day Sleeping
Beauty, her eyes closed to the outer world, her features in
perfect repose, her manner detached and reflective. In a circle
around her face, as if in her dreams, Francesco painted images
from Constance's poetry—a black enameled crow with one gold
eye, a rose, a magical door, a flock of white doves, a street corner in the middle of a snowfall, a golden butterfly.

He told me he'd taken his inspiration from R. W. Buss's
painting *Dickens's Dream*.

Constance's mother came to believe in the project whole-
heartedly. She even told me shyly when we were reviewing the
galleys that Constance had always promised to dedicate her first
book to her, so before we went to press we added, "To my
mother," after the title page.

Linda, my assistant, brought me the first copy.

"It's beautiful, Morgan. The jacket is amazing."

I opened the book and heard the spine crack pleasingly and the heavy pages rustle under my fingertips.

"Thank you, Linda," I said.

"Should I take a copy down to Matt?" she asked.

I nodded. "Yes, thank you."

Fifteen minutes later Matt appeared in my doorway. "Excellent dust jacket, Morgan. Who designed this?"

I told him.

"Has he done other books for us?"

"He did the Abélard and Héloise cover."

"Oh, right. We should submit it for some awards. Might as well try to get some recognition."

"Might as well," I said.

"It's an achievement. You should be proud of it."

"Oh, I am."

He lowered his head and studied his black wingtips. "She was one of a kind."

"Yes, one of a kind."

He looked up at me then, and for a moment we were comrades again rather than boss and underling. Sorrow hung heavy in the air like damp sheets. We stared at each other as if the weight of this loss bound us inescapably. Then a shroud of formality fell over his face again, and he excused himself.

After he left, I swiveled my chair around to face the bustling streets below filled with gift-laden Christmas shoppers and harried businesspeople. The music of goodwill greetings and chiming cash registers was in the air. A few vagrant snowflakes, exhausted from their descent through the heavens, melted away before anyone noticed them.

For a long while, I sat there pondering the curious events

of the previous year and contemplating that inextinguishable gleam in Constance's eyes whenever she talked about poetry or her love for Lou. That golden enthusiasm, that bright anticipation—that was life, I thought, in its purest form. I doubted I would ever again meet anyone as devoted as she had been to the ideals of truth: truth revealed, truth examined, truth illuminated for the first time. This seemed to be the constant in her life. Truth led to transformations of the soul; like a seed bursting its hard shell beneath the dark, life-giving nutrients of the earth, it effected eternal change.

But as she had acknowledged that day at the Waldorf, it was an acquired taste. A taste I assumed it had taken even her a while to acquire, if anything could be read into her poems and her elusive, shadowy past. But she had been learning.

"There is an implacable desire in the human heart to repeat the past at all costs," she'd said. A desire, I knew now, so profound that even the most vigilant among us succumb with amazing regularity. After all, hadn't I, in my own life as an editor, simply picked up where my father left off? Hadn't I spent my entire professional life panning for gold in the wide, shallow literary rivers of America? And hadn't Constance fallen into a relationship with Lou where, as in the one with her father, she was sure to lose in the end?

After spending months sorting through the hundreds of poems Constance had written, I'd come away with the overwhelming sense of an individual who, despite her powers of articulation, was struggling with a past she couldn't fully grasp, the effects of which were so pervasive she could not transcend them. As much as she talked about Lou repeating his own past, it seemed to me that she had done the same thing, and I think part of her knew this. As she wrote in one of her long poems:

> Eyes wander when a forgotten loss is met.
> Summer's incipient storms quickly pass into
>   memory
> Where they're hardly ever transformed.
> Shadows remain shadows,
> And the mind sits in its familiar uniform.
> The world passes by,
> And the heart fails to recognize a single sunrise.
> Love when it comes is misunderstood.

Maybe if she'd had more time. Perhaps she would have come to see Lou more realistically. Perhaps she would have seen the pattern her own unconscious desires were weaving. Perhaps she would have "extinguished the moonbeams" and opened up her heart a little more to outsiders. It was hard to say. But the poems she'd left behind seemed to be pointing in this direction. Metamorphosis, anyway, had been on her mind.

> The caterpillar isn't the only one
> Who experiences metamorphosis.
> I change form.
> It's gradual,
> Then I turn
> And I'm different from before,
> And everyone in my view is slightly altered.
> It's a lot more than becoming beautiful;
> That's what butterflies are for.

A Dialogue in Silence, published within a year of the author's death, found a wide audience. We sold forty thousand copies, a huge success for a poetry book. The reviewers said they hadn't seen anything like it in years and praised her "singular use of the feminine point of view." They were, I thought, almost too quick to praise these poems by a woman who had stepped outside the bounds of convention and paid for it with her life. And I wondered how much the world had changed. I had never expected to end up like Emily Dickinson's Higginson, the editor of a poet who was no longer here to enjoy her success. That had not been the point. That had not been the point at all.

About the Author

CATHERINE CANTRELL is a graduate of Duke University.
She lives in New York City.

About the Type

This book was set in Monotype Dante, a typeface designed by Giovanni Mardersteig (1892–1977). Conceived as a private type for the Officina Bodoni in Verona, Italy, Dante was originally cut only for hand composition by Charles Malin, the famous Parisian punch cutter, between 1946 and 1952. Its first use was in an edition of Boccaccio's *Trattatello in laude di Dante* that appeared in 1954. The Monotype Corporation's version of Dante followed in 1957. Though modeled on the Aldine type used for Pietro Cardinal Bembo's treatise *De Aetna* in 1495, Dante is a thoroughly modern interpretation of that venerable face.